# AGENT OF THE EMPIRE

## Red Dawn II

1 mile

# Imperial City, 210 Y.E.

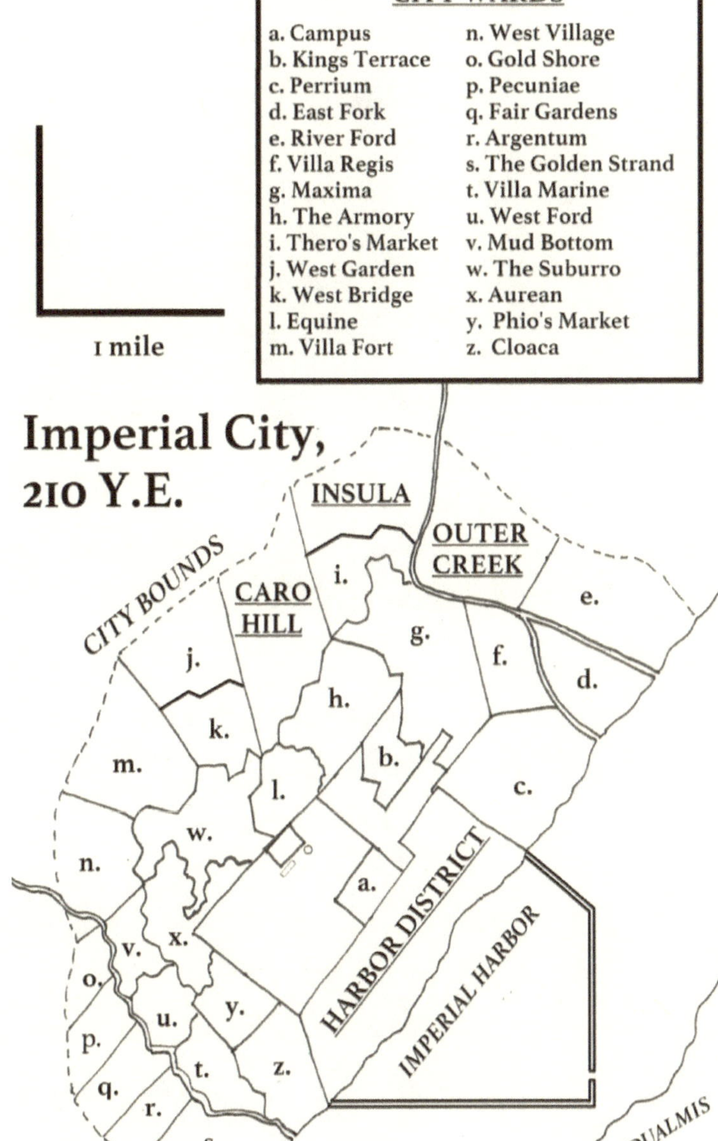

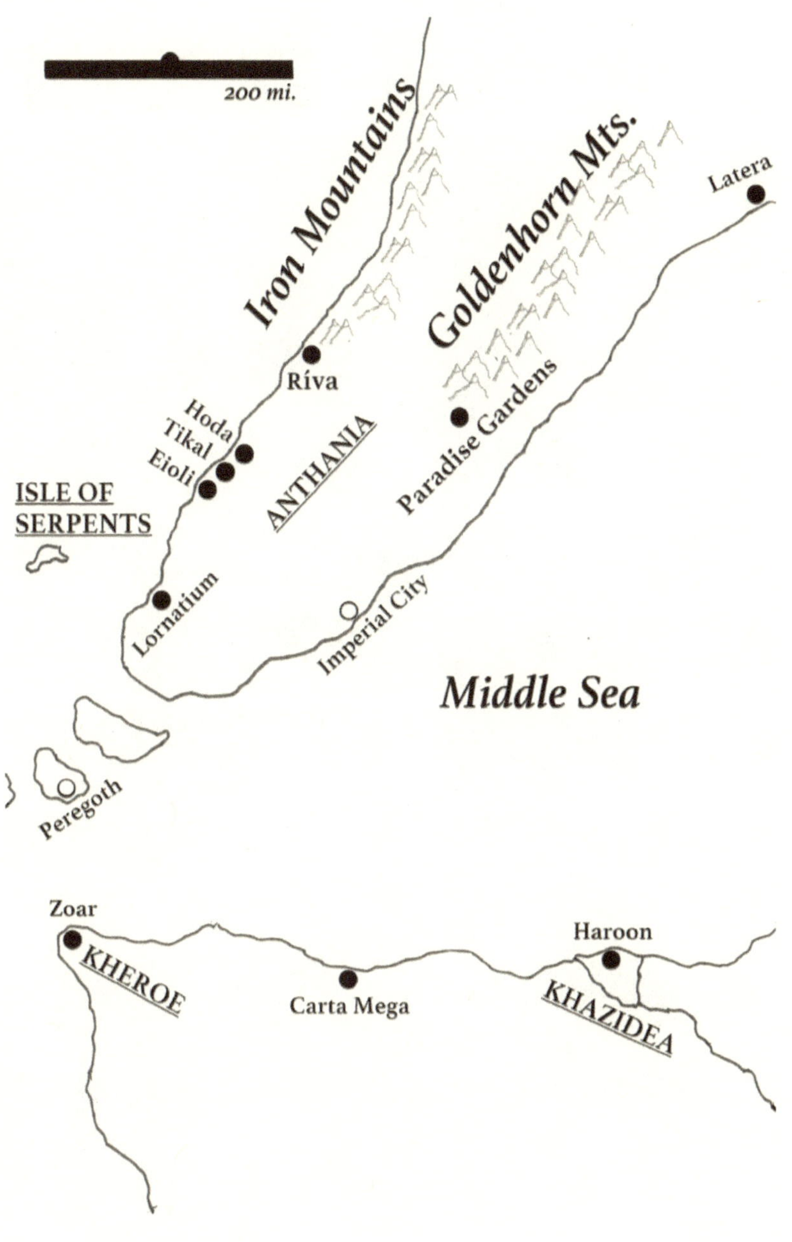

200 mi.
Iron Mountains
Goldenhorn Mts.
Latera
Ríva
Hoda
Tikal
Eioli
ISLE OF SERPENTS
ANTHANIA
Paradise Gardens
Lornatium
Imperial City
Middle Sea
Peregoth
Zoar
Haroon
KHEROE
Carta Mega
KHAZIDEA

# The Red Lord

The Red Lord did not recognize himself; when he looked in the mirror he saw that he was changed, and his heart was not still, he was full of passion and fire. His eyes were like coals, but fires were lighting in them.

He resolved to finish what Maria Domina started; she had transformed his prey, but where she had cursed, he would destroy.

# Part One

# Chapter One

*Publius Allius Corvus, Legionary*

The coach was rattling along the streets, and lights were filtering into its windows.

Publius Corvus had not had a good night's rest since he departed Forward Camp. The journey had been impossibly long; it had taken him through desolate scrub forests and burning hot plains, through roads and deer-paths forgotten by man. Eventually, the coach had merged onto the great white highway which pierced the peninsula and divided it into its eastern and western halves.

But now… now he looked out the window and he could see places he recognized, places that had—during the time of his training as a legionary—become nothing more than memories.

The stone buildings and concrete apartments of Mud Bottom surrounded him.

Here it was, the ward of Imperial City where he had grown up. It was among the poorest of all city wards, named after its location along the river. Here, tens of thousands of souls were crammed together in the poorest conditions that city regulators would allow.

And there were good memories here. He was passing the park where he would play in the summer, hiding behind bushes and hoping that his friend Tiverius wouldn't find him. But hide-and-seek was far from his mind, and he wished he were here for better reasons.

No, he was not here to celebrate or reminisce. He was here for his father Caius Corvus, for his father, who had died.

The Corvus family had been among the wealthier families of Mud Bottom, and compared to the countless throngs packed into apartments they were lucky.

Publius' stomach was twisting to knots as the coach rattled through the road, as it passed by Crooked Street and Mercers' Street, Cotters' Street and Butchers' Row. The streets were like an hourglass full of sand, diminishing slowly but surely until Publius reached the house on Seafarers' Way, where he had grown up, where he would have to face his childhood and the siblings he had not spoken to in years.

"Father," Publius mumbled under his breath, "why did you have to die?"

Tears began to well in his eyes anew. His lip began to quiver.

*Not this again.*

He had cried already, far too many times, and he had thought his tears had all been spent, but there were apparently some left.

"Father," Publius said. "Caius Corvus…tailor…Seafarers' Way."

In his old age he had become infirm, and unable to run the tailors' shop. He had left the shop in its entirety to Publius' brother, Marcus. That was why Publius had joined the legion; that was why he wore a red-and-gold tabard over his plainclothes. That was why he was riding in a government coach.

He wiped his eyes and the anxieties returned, his brother Marcus, his sister Flavia, his little sister Marcella—what were they doing with their lives, now? Mother had passed on long ago, and he had not spoken to his siblings in a long time, not since he took up the arms of a legionary and was sent to Blue Eagle Camp.

The house on Seafarers' Way was now a place he dreaded, but his father had to be honored… his father…

Like that, the tears began again. He could no longer look at Mud Bottom's streets; he could no longer look at their crooked edges, their dilapidated angles. He could no longer anticipate; he could no longer prepare.

And so, with a shout, the coachman announced that they had arrived, and within moments, the door was open, the black-garbed government official who had guided them was standing there, and Publius was furiously wiping his eyes, trying to shed all emotion, trying to shed all outward sign of pain.

"Three days are allotted to you, legionary," the official said. "Three days, and then you will be met here, at this spot, at high noon."

The siege of Eioli seemed a world away, and though its effects could alter history, to Publius they seemed petty now, as petty as anything. Caius Corvus, tailor, patriarch, was dead.

He stepped out at the open gate of the little house on Seafarer's Way.

For the most part, it was identical to how it had looked before, but to Publius' eyes the plaster seemed darker, the red roof tiles a little duller, having lost their lively luster.

But everything was a little darker now, everything a little more difficult, a little more challenging. The grief around him was like a stone around his neck; but he saw a face in the first-story window, the glint of eyes, and for a moment the burden dissipated. He walked through the open gate, into the little house on Seafarers' Way.


But when he entered, the main hall was empty. The home smelled musty. When Caius gave Publius' brother the family business to his indignation, he had assumed the home was transferred too. But perhaps, it was too small for Marcus, who'd always had dreams of wealth and ostentation, the desire for high society, for a grander position, perhaps for public office.

Publius walked to the parlor, where he'd seen those two dark eyes looking out from the window.

There was nothing there, only a divan, a round table lined

with a film of dust, and several lamps with dried-out wicks.

The seats looked like they hadn't been sat in for a long while.

Was it possible that Publius, a legionary who'd been stationed far away, in Ugarit, was here first, that his siblings had not arrived yet?

Commotion echoed upstairs, something tumbling from its place, followed by footsteps, then laughter. He recognized the voice as that of his sister Flavia.

He was not alone, no, no, he was not in fact the only one who cared. He was not the favored son and he'd never be. In answer to the voice, he hurried out of the room, up a familiar set of stairs that had always creaked when he ascended them. He remembered those stairs, those worn wooden steps that never failed to make noise, this staircase that led to the upper level, to his private chamber, where he'd spent his childhood.

There was an upper parlor overlooking the street, and there he found his siblings, two of them at least: Flavia and Marcella.

They had changed only a little in appearance; Flavia was still blonde and beautiful, Marcella darker and more somber.

"Publius!" Flavia said and stood up.

She was garbed in a gown of scarlet, and jewels were on the rings of her fingers.

Publius heard she had married a rich man, but seeing her like this was stunning to him, and not altogether good.

"Publius!" Flavia said again, and met him in a light embrace.

Strong perfume hovered over her, the scent of pine and something else, some other pungent material.

"Flavia," Publius said. "It is good to see you."

He had not attended the wedding; it had occurred not long after he first went to Blue Eagle Camp. But he had heard her husband was a manager of businesses in Imperial Harbor, a dealer in tar or ambergris or some obscure good.

Marcella stood up to greet him, eyes twinkling, and Publius saw that she was no longer wearing a ring on her finger. Moreover, she was dressed in plain brown clothes she'd not have been caught dead in, not even in her impoverished youth. And there was a wimple she was wearing, a head covering she had removed to bare her hair.

"Publius," Marcella said, and kissed him on the lips.

"Your ring…" Publius said.

"Alexus and I have parted ways," said Marcella. "And I have committed myself to the gods. The convent allowed me leave to honor Father."

His sister Marcella… a vestal. Stranger things had occurred, he supposed, but in his youth, growing up in Mud Bottom, she had acquired a sordid reputation. Now she was a changed woman, but Publius didn't realize that convents permitted divorced women to take the vows.

"It is good to see you all," Publius said, though he did not in his heart wish to see them, to open up old resentments, old wounds. "And Marcus…" he said.

"Marcus is on business in Khazidea," Flavia answered in turn. "A ship was sent to alert him. He will be home any day now, I suppose."

Flavia brushed Publius' shoulder with her white hand. "And you… you are decked in the Empire's finest. Your hair cut short. A tabard of red and gold. I am sure you have no problem attracting women."

That was not why he was there, or why any of them were there. He had left the siege for this, to honor his father, to honor his father only.

In truth, deep within his heart, he had looked forward to the day of battle, to proving himself, to showing the world and the nation that he was useful. But that had been taken from him.

And here he was, with a black cloud over him, a pain deep

within. His father… he had not stopped to think, to dwell, to reminisce. He had spent the days in the coach in a place between boredom and grief, with no restfulness, no time to ponder. His father, Caius Corvus, expert tailor, the owner of the only private house on Seafarers' Way, had gone on to see the gods.

He turned to Flavia and looked into her blue eyes, seeing that pain had settled within them, though it was faint to see. He clasped her hand in his, and felt that it was cold. "Flavia," he said, "where are you staying?"

"With my husband of course," Flavia said. "You should come with me and stay with me. This house has too many memories. And now Father is not in it."

Publius would take up Flavia on her offer, of that he was sure.

And then, when he had decided, he thought again of when he had first arrived, how he had seen two dark eyes peering through the window. Who was it, he wondered. On closer pondering, he did not think it was either of his sisters.

# Chapter Two

*Varius Tycho, Legionary*

The city of Eioli lay before Tycho, surrounded by Imperial camps.

It was as large as he had heard, and though a constant percussion of catapults had damaged the wall, still its beauty stuck out to Tycho in the sunlight.

The walls were colored gold, the color of a summer afternoon. In places, the votive statues of the city god could be seen, a bull's head with a ring in its nose.

Tycho thought he had seen it all. He had been to Zoar, the city of stone, one of the Empire's closest allies; but even there he had not seen something so strange. Eioli and the sister cities—those cities of the coast, of Ugarit, which had broken free from the Empire's influence—were in a league of their own, and even now in the sunlit day, Tycho could not help but feel a sense of fear, of nightmare.

Ugarit was so close to the Empire in distance, within a week's journey from Imperial City if you rode fast enough. But its customs were strange, and in the camps rumors had begun to spread of human sacrifice, of practices so foreign and so immoral they shocked even the Empire's soldiers. But like the other soldiers, Tycho had never seen anything quite like this, the carvings of the "god" Belpheor on the walls, the rhythmic chants which the defenders would sing, and above all, the unwillingness of the Empire's own appointed grand legate—Agatho Lornodoris—to do anything about it. Ugarit was a land of myth and nightmare, possessing rich soil but also deep-rooted fear.

And in his now twenty years in the legion Tycho had seen much. He had not only gone to the stone city of Zoar but also to her sister, to the red city of Haroon, where—on leave—he had spent nights in spice dens and opium parlors, where he had tasted the forbidden fruits of intoxicating plants and substances. He had availed himself of Haroon's brothels where—gods help him—he had acquired Red Itch, for which there was no known cure.

And yet still, staring at this city, which not long ago had dwarfed the Imperial capital, he still realized there was nothing like this place or these people, these anomalies of the peninsula, the Ugars.

There was no fighting on the walls, though the grand legate had set up siege equipment. The watchers on the walls did not loose their arrows, and Tycho—though he had seen much over his career—had a feeling of unease he could not shake, a feeling something terrible was going to happen. But he had felt such a way before, and had it not come to pass.

Tycho adjusted his armor.

He had seen so much. He was approaching age forty. By rights he could retire, but he had not, for what would he do with his time? He was a man of war and nothing else.

A trumpet blew, a loud crisp peal. It was coming from the distance.

Tycho turned and spotted horses riding to camp, and on the horses men wearing the red and gold tabards of the Empire. These were messengers sent from Imperial City. All along the main highway such persons were posted, allowing letters to be carried in a relay, one horse galloping after the other, reducing the time of message delivery to mere days. From their lofty seats in the Council House, the Imperial Council could manage the Sixth Anthanian from afar, to demand that they honor this or that regulation, to manage the war effort from a distance.

Old men they were, doddering fools, and few had experience with war.

And now the whole of the Empire was controlled by those

thirty men. The Empire was under council rule, and the White Throne sat empty.

"Tycho!" He recognized the voice of his friend Hatius.

He was approaching, Hatius. The legionary was half Tycho's age; he had just joined. Tycho had taken him under his wing and shown him the arts of war, how to wield his shield this or that way, how to bear up in times of battle, to lock shields together. Hatius was untested, but Tycho had a good feeling about him, as good a feeling as he'd had about any green recruit.

"What do you think is the delay?" Hatius said.

Was he eager to start the siege, or did he wish only to stop worrying, to begin what he feared and have it over with? The nerves of battle never left you, but Tycho exulted in it now—it was a thrill and not a burden.  When he had been a green recruit, battle had made him fear; but not now.

"Do not worry, Hatius," Tycho said. "It will all be all right."

Of course, Tycho did not know that; the Fourth Peregothian had broken on the Ugars like a pack of cowards.

But in Hatius Tycho saw a little of himself, of his old self, when he was more innocent and more pure, before the years of hard drinking and other vices wore him down. He hoped Hatius would not make the same mistakes, but they were everywhere for the legionary, tempting him at every turn.

Hatius said nothing for a while. "Have you had dreams?" he eventually uttered, and as if in answer a wind began to blow, a cold wind with just a hint of winter.

Tycho heard stories of nightmares befalling the legionaries, of eyes in darknesses, of fear and the worry that—while they were sleeping—they were not alone.

But Tycho had not been touched by them, and what's more, he knew that the stresses of war affected everyone differently, and that some reacted in strange ways. Not all were fit for the legion, but by the time they learned it was too late.

"No," Tycho said. "No dreams. Do not worry, Hatius. We will crush Eioli. We will bring them to heel."

He spoke no lie; in his heart he could feel it. He could sense it. One day soon, Eioli would pay a price for its insolence. One day soon, the gates of the city would break and the three legions would come storming in. The Ugars would rue the day they rebelled, the day they went against their word. They would regret their actions. And the Empire would prevail.

Hatius turned and slipped away. He was a slender figure in the waning sunlight. The years had not worn on him; he had not been afflicted like Tycho had, and as the winter wind blew, Tycho uttered something not unlike a prayer, to whatever god would hear him, that Hatius would not see what Tycho had seen, that he would not do what Tycho had done, that when Hatius reached the age of forty he would be innocent and without regret.

But Tycho knew the chances of that were slim.

~

The sun was setting and a campfire had been built. The fire was burning away the wood, and the night's chill was waning. More shipments of food had arrived, salted pork and beef, waybread, watered-down wine.

And in the flickering light of the fire Tycho looked across, and saw that his centurion was approaching.

Pius was a little older than Tycho, no nobleman, not an August or a Knight. But he had earned his position; that was for sure, and while Tycho had improved little beyond the humble rank of legionary, Pius had used his years to advance.

In the light of the fire, Pius stretched his right finger, beckoning Tycho silently.

The night was dark, and wind was on the hills. Everywhere

there seemed a note of dolour, and the silence of the city defenders, the lack of battle, made all seem worse.

About a dozen other legionaries were there on the hill with Tycho, plus Pius, but the city was drawing his attention, a dark outline in the distance, and the glow of lamps and fireplaces. Tycho wondered if Agatho Lornodoris—the grand legate—was, in his poor estimation, intent on starving the city out. But Tycho knew the soil was rich, and that Eioli was well supplied. It might be more than a year before they broke.

"Congratulations," Pius said in the midst of the night noises, the crickets chirping, the wind gently gusting. "You have been chosen for a special task, the ten of you. You are the most experienced and elite of your centuries, and I am placing you under the command of the most senior of you—Varius Tycho."

Tycho looked at Pius in astonishment. He supposed it was no surprise. He had seen it all; he had been in more battles and sieges than he could count.

"The Imperial Council has personally approved this special operation," Pius said. "For our spies have uncovered something. An informant tells us there is a secret passage into the city, into Eioli. It is more than a mile away, obscured by brush. Your mission is to quietly enter and make sure not to attract attention. You are to gather information about the city, to identify its weaknesses. Then you are to quietly return the way you have come."

The mission sounded deceptively simple, but Tycho knew it would be extraordinarily difficult. These ten men were now at great risk to their lives, for if caught the Ugars were notorious for their cruelty. And it was Tycho's charge to get them quickly in and out.

Tycho had risked death before, in missions such as this. But as he looked on the dark outline of the city walls, and the lights that glowed above it, he felt his stomach twist to knots, and an uncharacteristic fear develop deep in his gut. Eioli was a city of darkness and dark enchantment, and no one here had ever seen its like. The Ugars did not let in foreigners, least of all Imperials. They would glimpse things no outsider was meant to glimpse; they were to observe things no one besides Ugars had observed before.

"Mission accepted," Tycho said, and the rest of the soldiers began to grunt their approval. Perhaps they'd had no choice, but affirmation was important; Tycho wanted to project confidence that he did not have. The mission may be suicide but nerves would increase the chances of disaster.

No doubt these legionaries were the best of the best, experienced in tasks of stealth. But Eioli... Eioli was a different beast altogether, and no one here knew her. That was why they were being sent.

Eioli. The heart of it.

In his older years, Tycho had begun to think more on the gods. Perhaps, this time, before he departed, he would ask for their aid.

# Chapter Three

*Constantius Pello, Speaker in Absentia*

The Sky Bridge connected the Imperial Palace to its superior, the Council House.

Constantius Pello was standing upon it, and the night wind was kissing his cheek.

Below, the city stretched from the harbor into the interminable distance. The lights of the homes and the shops were like beacons, so numerous in number it was difficult to distinguish the individual points.

Fall was coming; summer was almost over. The air was gentle and cool.

And the Empire, for many months now, had been under Council rule.

As Constantius stood there, surveying the stars, he pondered this thought and what it meant. The emperor, the occupant of the White Throne, had gained more and more power since the nation's founding, and the checks on his power had steadily eroded. It was written in the tablets of law that the powers of the emperor arose from the Council, and the powers of the Council arose from the people. So it had been, and so it would be.

The emperors had not managed to crush the Ugar uprising. The emperors had not conquered Eioli. But under Council rule, the war effort continued, and the rebellious cities had begun to show signs of strain. Friends of the Empire they were—so they had pledged—and pledges could not be revoked. Friends of the Empire they would remain until the Empire crumbled, or until the world itself ended.

As Constantius stood there in the brisk air, seeing the waters of the harbor glint with moonlight, he realized just how fortunate he was. His fellow councilor, Agatho Lornodoris, was the Speaker, but under the laws of Council rule he was therefore the commander-in-chief. So it was he and not the emperor leading the armies. And Constantius, ruling in his stead, had become his replacement. As Speaker in Absentia, he had the powers and none of the responsibilities.

And secretly, he had begun to think of what he could do with this power. He wondered how he could turn it to his, and to the Empire's advantage.

The moon was a thin crescent. The wind was refreshingly cool. And Constantius Pello, turning around, headed back to the Council House to make his way home.

~

To his surprise, when he reached the great domed Council Chambers, he saw that he was not alone. A shadowy figure was standing there in the almost total darkness. But what light he could see from the ever-burning lamps it was a councilor, a white robe over his body, a dark sash accenting it.

"Constantius," the councilor said. It was the voice of Junius Arappo, the councilor from West Garden.

As Constantius walked over, he felt his stomach twisting to knots. Proximity outlined Junius' features, the gray hair, the dark eyes, the pale lips. He was one of the lesser known councilors and did not often make his presence known when the Council was in session.

But why was he here, late at night?

Constantius had had business to take care of before the following morning; letters of sale and writs of permission to sign, things that required the signature of the Speaker, and therefore the Council, and therefore—for now, at least—the White Throne.

"Junius," Constantius said and bowed his head. "What are

you doing here?'

Junius' voice lowered to a whisper. "Have you heard… the rumor… the Strig?"

"The Strig?" Constantius said. "What is the Strig?"

"A Strig," Junius said, "is neither living nor dead. It feeds on the blood of humans. It has great prodigious fangs, and big black eyes. It remembers nothing of its former life… and some in the palace say they've seen one crawling up the Council Chambers in the moonlight."

Such a preposterous claim was difficult to take seriously, and like that Constantius' opinion of Junius was lowered.

"Perhaps, you are listening to too many scary tales," Constantius said.

"The Magister of Coin was working late last night," Junius said. "He claims to have seen it."

Strigs… ghosts… Constantius of course believed in the supernatural, in the powers of the gods above, but a Strig running rampant in the Council Chambers was too much.

But the Magister of Coin was a rational man, a believer in very little besides what he could see and observe with his own eyes. His name was Portius Sacco and if a witness were to be believed, he would be it.

"I am glad you are concerned," Constantius said. "But if you are intent on seeing the Strig, perhaps find a virgin in Imperial City—if one can be found—and tie her to the dome."

"Do not mock me," Junius answered. "You may not believe, but others claimed to have seen it too, not just the Magister of Coin."

In the darkness, Constantius for the first time noted that Junius was carrying a book.

It was a big tome, a codex with yellowed pages.

"What is that?" Constantius said.

"Here," Junius said, "read for yourself."

The moonlight was reflecting on the tome, a large book titled "Dark Incidents" by an anonymous author.

Outside, on the Sky Bridge, Constantius read its words.

On a large black page, writ in dark ink, was an entry titled "The Strig."

"Beware the Strig," the text read, "neither living nor dead nor undead. It has been cursed with undeath while still alive, and it hungers for blood. No more does it remember its name or its past life. It can be killed only by a silver dagger, and only then if it is beheaded and its mouth stuffed with garlic."

If Junius thought this would convince Constantius, he was sorely mistaken. The idea seemed more outlandish than ever.

"Well," Constantius began, "I'll leave you to your pursuits. I hope you find what you are looking for."

Junius was glaring when he turned to leave.


But Constantius, as he departed the Council Chambers and headed down its winding staircases, had to admit that he was frightened, that every turn of a shadow, every flicker of the lamp, might indicate the presence of one of those warped entities, the Strigs that the common people feared.

He kept those thoughts to himself, and reminded himself that the Council Guard was posted at all hours. Perhaps the Strig would mistake their steel swords for silver knives.

But a big day was planned tomorrow, a grand morning. It was there he would reward his patron. As the councilor for Kings Terrace, he represented the richest of the city's wards, the epicenter of the Empire's wealth, where all the money from taxation and war eventually ended up.

~

The subterranean tunnels beneath the Council chambers led Constantius home, and eventually expelled him up above-ground into Kings Terrace.

It was late, and his meeting was set for the tenth hour after noon, at a time when every respectable citizen would be in bed. Constantius did not like to deal with shady characters or miscreants of any kind—it was beneath his pedigree—but if he didn't would he ever build his own villa in Paradise Gardens? Would the House of Pello ever outshine the storied families of the Seáni and Kerii?

Even in the night, the ward of Kings Terrace emanated wealth.

Its white streets were swept immaculately clean; there was not a trace of filth or dirt to the perfectly-fitted stones. The raised walkways were lined with colonnades, and the manors of the rich were everywhere, on every street corner, towering in size but not crowding out the sky like the filthy apartments of the poor. Manhole covers dotted the white streets; every home was connected via lead pipe to running water.

Constantius was blessed to live here, even if he were not lucky to represent the haughty denizens of Kings Terrace. Their demands were never ending. That was the problem with democracy. If one wanted to survive, you had to become the public's servant.

Better the time of kings, when noblemen did not fear the people, but instead the common feared those who governed them. Better the time when the Council served as advisors to a monarch and little else, and their pronouncements and resolutions were not tinged with the worry that came with responsibility. In those days, the Council had been advisors and nothing more—wealthy advisors, but advisors nonetheless.

Constantius turned. At the turn of the tenth hour, the temple bells would ring; then they would remain silent for the remainder of the night.

It was at a pavilion on "Kings Way" that he was meeting this character, this character who called himself "Gray Hood" but whose veracity had been vouched for.

The night deepened, the bells rang, and Constantius found the pavilion at last, a little late but not terribly so.

In the distance, street lamps were flickering, offering a dull glow.

The person underneath the pavilion, the one who called himself "Gray Hood," who had titillated Constantius with an underhanded proposal, was standing there. He represented his namesake well. A gray hood was laid upon his head, and his silvery eyes were twinkling. His lips were pallid. When he spoke, a raspy voice emerged, the voice of one who had smoked too many pipes in the manner of the southrons.

"Constantius," he said.

It was a lower class accent, not surprising, he supposed, but still unexpected. In Kings Terrace, only servants and those who lived outside the ward spoke in such a manner.

"You are Gray Hood." Constantius was soon near him, underneath the pavilion. In the distance, there was the faint sound of drums and music, the noise of a night party perhaps. Constantius had been invited to many such parties before he became a councilor, but not now.

Gray Hood adjusted his cloak, then let the hood fall off his head.

Constantius took a step back at the sight: an old and mottled face, covered in whiskers, with a soupy white eye that surely couldn't see. Gray Hood was hunched over a bit, and indeed he reeked of pipe smoke. His hand was trembling, but at his side Constantius could see a dagger.

"You... spoke of a deal," Constantius began, and found

that his voice was wavering. Suddenly, he was unsure of this proposition, and he wondered what his friends in the government were thinking when they vouched for him. Constantius was unprotected, without a weapon in hand, and how easily Gray Hood's dagger could slide into him like butter. How easily Constantius could fall victim to this thug.

"A deal, yes," Gray Hood said. "And do not be alarmed. I've come on behalf of my superior. I am merely the messenger."

Perhaps, Gray Hood could sense the fear and disdain within Constantius. Many of the common did not react well to that on the faces of their betters.

"A deal," Gray Hood said. "You provide us with the law… and you get back twenty percent."

These shadowy figures wanted to add construction to the Council House, to update its hallways and corridors and to build a large façade stretching out into the street. Their request made little sense, but Constantius believed the Council would take well to it, and the builders—who would overcharge them—would provide Constantius with a generous kickback. Twenty percent of one-hundred twenty thousand sovereigns would do Constantius well; it would allow him to fulfill all his dreams of villas and private islands and gardens floating in the sea. The Pello family and not the Kerius family would be, then, the richest of the Augusts.

"We shall sign a contract," Gray Hood said.

"No," Constantius said. "This is on faith. We will leave no paper footprint."

Gray Hood looked disappointed.

But he was a fool if he thought there were going to be any contracts to sign. Yes, the councilors did shady deals, sometimes in the open, but what Constantius was embarking upon had a whiff of illegality. He could surely squash the investigation by the aediles but not at great cost to his reputation, perhaps to his conciliar career.

"Very well," Gray Hood said. "Have it your way. But how

can we trust you?"

"Trust me?" Constantius said. "I will be the one pressing for this absurd construction project. It will cost me much. It is I who must trust you… and if you don't deliver, why, Signor Gray Hood, you will learn what crossing a Pello means."

Gray Hood mumbled something indistinguishable. "We wait for news of the passage of the law. You will hear from us then. We will make arrangements for payment."

He paused a moment.

"So it is agreed… tonight, on this, the fifteenth of Harona," Gray Hood said. "We make our contract by speaking."

"It is agreed," Constantius said. "You will have your blueprints drawn up, and I will receive my recompense."

In a moment's span, Gray Hood turned and walked away, vanishing into the dim lights of Kings Terrace.

Up above, the moon was shining, colored ochre, almost red.

# Chapter Four

*Publius Allius Corvus, Legionary*

When he heard Flavia married rich, Publius had expected something grand, but not this.

The home where Flavia lived overlooked the harbor, and right when you walked through the open double doors, you were in a vast great hall. An immense glass window, covering much of the wall, overlooked the moonlit waters of the sea. Before the great window were divans and seats lined with linens, tables with partially-drunk goblets, and portraits of Flavia and her husband Demetrius.

Demetrius was polite enough.

He was young, too young to be a self-made man of such wealth. He couldn't be much older than Publius, and at the thought there was an unwelcome twinge of jealousy.

Demetrius was dark; his hair was almost black, his eyes the color of almonds, his skin a dark olive complexion.

He was rich, but Publius purged himself of his jealousy and walked forward.

"You've really moved up," he said to Flavia, though she was now behind him.

He walked up to the edge of the great hall, to the window, and saw the waters of the harbor glinting in the moonlight. He looked up, to the moon, and saw it was reddish-gold, almost bronze.

The augurs and omen-takers would have no end to their speculation tonight.

He sensed Flavia behind him; it was the whiff of perfume surely.

"And you've moved up," Flavia said, "in a different way.

You bear the arms and armor of the nation. You are what allows Demetrius and I to have this charmed life."

It was something every soldier had heard before, something everyone said. On the streets of Imperial City, sometimes people would thank him. But war was far from the capital; its pains and terrors were a world away, here in this place of luxury and dark entertainments.

Flavia drew near him, touched his hand. He turned and looked into her eyes. They were blue, blue as the cloudless sky. But Publius saw weariness in them, weariness beyond their father's death.

"Tell me of your exploits," Flavia said. "Have you seen battle?"

"No," Publius said. "I was posted in Eioli. Then the news came."

Demetrius was approaching. There were rings on his fingers. He had over his chest a jet-black tunic of wool embroidered in gold. His breeches were of fustian, colored white. His hair was neatly shorn, his face as hairless as a baby's; evidently he could afford a good barber.

"Eioli, hmm?" Demetrius said. "You were there? The city of the Ugars?

"What do you think of the war? Do you think it is justified? Do you think we have a right to order them around?"

"I'd rather not talk about it," Publius said. "In fact, I think I ought to sleep."

~

The bed they provided was in the upper story, a small room with a foggy window that looked out into the streets of the harbor. Beside the bed was a bookshelf full of curious tomes, books of geography and history and medicine. There was even a copy of the epic of the Megarine war, as told by the poet Arkelaios.

But reading he did not want. He wanted to rest, if at all possible. He had had trouble sleeping ever since he heard the news about Father, and grief and anxiety had mixed a toxic potion in his heart.

But he would try to rest, yes, he would try; one sibling was last to arrive, Marcus, whom Publius had often envied. After facing Marcus, facing the Ugars would be nothing.

# Chapter Five

*Publius Allius Corvus, Legionary*

Publius shot up out of bed. He was dripping in cold sweat, and his tunic was wet.

The lingering fear of a nightmare hovered over him.

There was a tapping on the window outside, through the foggy glass, a loud cackle, then a dark face taking shape, a being making its presence known.

It tapped on the window with a long claw, then scraped against the glass.

And through the glass of the window, though the face was dark, he made out traces of blond hair, a shape he recognized, though he couldn't place it.

What was this thing? Climbing the roof of Flavia's house was no easy task.

And the figure before him acted strangely, precariously. It seemed to almost float in the air, and had little control of its hands.

Yes, it was human in shape, but he could tell it was not human, not at all; it was both gangly and bloated, and though the window was shut a bit of air was seeping through, and the smell of a rancid corpse.

He had heard tales of the "living dead," of ghosts and revenants and corpses returned to false life. He had not believed, but now, now something was just inches from him across the window-glass.

"What are you?" Publius said despite his fear, and pressed a finger to the window.

The creature hissed something indistinguishable and drew back, then swiftly floated forward.

"Publius…" it said. "Publius…"

Somehow it knew his name. Gods help him. He turned around and hurried to the corner of the room, where he had laid his things. He picked up his sheath and drew out his legionary's sword.

He ran to the window, intending to open it and confront the creature, but it was gone, completely vanished, as if the wind had carried it away.

The creature knew his name… it was hunting him.

Flavia and Demetrius were in danger.

So, setting his sword aside, he donned some rude clothing, then buckled the sheath to his belt. He headed outside.

~

The wind was blowing, and in the distance was the faint sound of whitecaps crashing to shore.

The moon by now had lost much of its reddish tint; higher in the sky it was now, a crescent.

The streets of Imperial City were all about him. Across from the home was a warehouse where, no doubt, goods from all over the world were stored.

And he was not alone, no, not in the slightest sense of the word. Underneath the lamplight, it seemed the day had not ended; drunken sailors were stumbling down the way. In the distance were prostitutes wearing tunics and nothing else.

Publius walked forward into the street and looked up to his bedroom window, where the creature had been.

The roof was towering, at a harsh angle, and there was no easy way to scale it, nor was there a ladder that the creature could have used. Somehow it had leapt from an adjoining house, or found some other way to climb.

And though it was there not long ago, it was gone; there was no trace of it, and as Publius stood there in the dark street, the longer he lingered the less safe he felt. There were robbers aplenty in the harbor district, the city's least safe ward, and though Flavia and Demetrius lived in the best part, crime was no doubt still present.

Whoever said not to fear the night was wrong, for things do live in the night which do not live in the day—criminals and those who seek to harm, and those who do not want their deeds to come to light.

"Hey! You there!" A prostitute was approaching, holding her tunic down against the wind.

And like that Publius bolted inside, all fear of the undead creature gone. There were things worse than the undead, and more frightful, and they lived in the open in Harbor District.

# Chapter Six

*Publius Allius Corvus, Legionary*

The morning light was filtering into the main hall.

Outside, through the glass of the window, the harbor was in view, a crystal blue color, and the sky was clear and cloudless.

It was a beautiful day, yes, a beautiful day; but now when he woke the sadness lingered.

He was alone; Flavia and Demetrius were nowhere in sight.

He had only his grief, the memory of Caius Corvus who had been taken from him.

And resentments lingered also, resentments of a son who was not favored. From his earliest days, Caius had doted on Marcus, buying him all manner of expensive things. On his thirteenth birthday, Caius had bought Marcus a splendid tunic of scarlet. And throughout his life Caius had encouraged Marcus, remarking on his intelligence, his wisdom, his hard work, ensuring him that he'd do well for himself.

And as for Publius, he had felt ignored.

When Caius Corvus, old and infirm, granted the family business to Marcus in its entirety, it had truly sealed the deal; it had truly made Publius aware of what his father taught him.

And it was because of that that there was a sword in his bedroom; it was because of that that Publius' hair was closely cropped and it was why, in a few days' time, that he would be heading northeastwards to Eioli to face victory or death.

But the window provided a picaresque view, and the waves were gently rolling in. Seagulls were circling up above the wharf, and in the waters ships of all shapes and sizes were sailing—great grain tankers from Khazidea, triremes and quadremes of the Imperial navy, and in the distance a southron dhow with a crimson sail.

All this wealth, all this commerce, and Publius knew just how much of it was trickling into the hands of the rich. His sister Flavia had married into it; her husband, he learned, dealt in tar and concrete, and managed not one or two but seventeen individual businesses. And what's more, he was younger than Publius, aged twenty-five. Already he'd seen more money than Father had saw in his lifetime, but if he had any shame about meeting with impoverished beggars from Mud Bottom he'd shown no sign of it.

Demetrius was rich but he was no Knight or August; there was no noble blood in him, and so certain things remained out of bounds, certain things would stay forever out of reach. He would never govern; he would never hold the positions of councilor or emperor or magister.

Publius exalted in that fact and tried to force a grin. Certain things were outside the reach of Demetrius, yes, his life was not perfect.

The dhow by now had turned, its dark crimson sail dragging the ship into a sudden new direction. It was veering to shore, and the dhow was large, the largest dhow Publius had ever seen.

He felt, for a reason he did not know, that he should go see it. And so hurriedly he ran upstairs to put on his cloak. An inexplicable force drove him forward and gave speed to his steps.

~

He breached the harbor walls and found himself in a different world; streets packed from one end to the other with crowds of people, sailors and workmen scurrying to and fro, crates being moved on cranes, carts filled with amphorae driving through the masses, draco sellers and wine merchants and foreigners from every coast in the world.

But Publius resolved to move forward, and so he pushed ahead, down the street, down the road, until he reached the docks. It would have been easy to lose track, but as soon as he pushed beyond the people he saw the dhow cruising across the blue waters.

He did not know why he was following the dhow, except a feeling he had, a desire deep within.

And so he pushed forward, aggressively, casting aside the people this way and that, until at last he found the dock where the dhow was.

A crew was there, of southrons in turbans and Khazideans in headwraps. The deck of the ship was loaded with crates.

He approached, walking down the dock, not knowing why. A wave crashed against the wood, and the foam sprayed against his cheek.

His brother emerged from the cabin, walking up the stairs, yes, his brother, Marcus Corvus.

He recognized him instantly, but time, it seemed, had worn him thin; wrinkles had developed on his face and though he was a man in his twenties there was some gray to his black hair, and much weariness to his eyes.

Some said Publius and Marcus looked exactly alike, but Publius had never seen it. "Brother!" he said. "Brother!"

But the noise of the harbor was too great, and Marcus was idling there on the deck.

Publius pressed forward. "Marcus…" he said, fainter this time, and then they exchanged glances, Publius on the dock, among the crowds, and Marcus standing on the deck of the dhow.

He did not so much as smile; he raised a hand to hail him, but his face was dark and somber.

Father had died, yes, but Marcus seemed shrunken almost, a lesser person than when he had last seen him.

So Publius idled there while the southron sailors tied the dhow to the docks.

Publius wondered what they were carrying and why his brother was on a ship of southron make.

It seemed Marcus was taking his time, that he did not want to leave the boat and enter the city. Perhaps, he did not want to face reality, the reality that his father was gone from this world.

But eventually he had to leave.

In time, Marcus was there before him, offering him a slight hug, and it was then that Publius noted a reddish tinge to Marcus' eyes.

"It is good to see you," Publius said.

Marcus smiled weakly in response. "Brother," he mumbled.

There was a slight limp to his walk and a harsh scent to his tunic.

*What,* Publius thought silently, *has happened to my brother?*

~

The news came like a wildfire, and he learned, between his walks with his brother and through the whispered words of his sisters that afternoon, that Marcus Corvus had lost the family business, that it had fallen all through his fingertips, that he had ventured off to Haroon and spent his fortune on iniquity.

He was not who Publius expected him to be; but Publius would be there for him.

# Chapter Seven

*Varius Tycho, Legionary*

The dusk was lying low over the hills, and the sun was casting long shadows over the trees, when Tycho made his approach to the trapdoor.

All had been exactly planned; all had been thoroughly thought through. But despite the men behind them, well-armed veterans of many fights, Tycho could not help but feel a whiff of fear, not the thrill of battle but an uncomfortable kind, a slowly growing dread, not of failure but of the mission itself, of what he might see in the city of Eioli, and what might happen to him there.

Ugars began to flee as soon as they reached them; three were guarding the gate to the hidden entrance. This had been expected.

Tycho lifted up his arm, raised two fingers.

Ventrius and Pellus, expert archers from the Second Peregothian Legion, ran forth with their bows, having already nocked arrows to the string.

They let loose a quick succession of arrows; one instantly plucked an Ugar in the back, and on the third volley the other two fell.

Tycho raised one finger. "Hurry," he muttered quietly under the haunting light of dusk.

Adrianus, an expert runner from the Sixth Anthanian, sprinted across the fields like a gazelle, and the others—including Tycho—followed him at half his pace.

Adrianus drew his dagger and one by one, silenced the Ugar's agonized screams. Bleeding they lay in the fields, against the waning afternoon sun. The mission had succeeded; and so it would commence.

Tycho raised three fingers, and the legionaries assembled—elite veterans, plucked from each of the legions. Silently, amid the oppressive heat, they got to work.

A pile of stones masked the trapdoor which led to the secret passage. Wordlessly they hauled them apart, piece by piece, until—underneath the long grass, obscured by a thin layer of dirt, the bronze knob of the door appeared.

Tycho lifted four fingers, and Tiverius—the largest of the bunch, a giant of a man, jerked at the locked door until it gave way with a crash.

This, Tycho knew, was the escape route for the city's elite, and a way of transporting messages to those inside.

But the Ugars were cowards, and an informant had told the Empire of everything. Such a people could not last long in war.

~

They would navigate the passage in darkness.

The most difficult part had been done, and it had been executed in perfection.

But for the coming hours, there would be only two participants: Tycho and Aulus.

Aulus, a veteran of the Second Peregothian, was stepping behind him in the blackness.

Verbal instructions had been made; they would use their minds and senses for navigation.

In the darkness, Tycho whispered, "Ready?"

Aulus touched Tycho's hand in answer, and together, slowly, step by step, they made their way through the passage.

Twice in his first few steps Tycho tripped, but managed not to utter curses.

The air was musty and thick.

But Tycho had been through worse. In his time in the

legions, he had navigated sandstorms and whirlwinds; at the behest of the Empire's ally Kheroe, he had crossed deserts. What was this, compared to that?

"Stop," Aulus said audibly and Tycho looked back, as if expecting to see him, or anything.

A spark burst into existence, then a blazing torch. Tycho wanted to curse his partner out, but then he saw there was a great pit in front of him, just steps away, and at the bottom spikes coated with viscous black fluid.

"How did you…" Tycho began, but he stopped himself. His heart was pounding in his chest. He had been an inch from death.

"A change of plans," he went on. "We use lights."

~

Many more pits there were to step over, traps of all kinds, as if they had prepared for intruders.

But even here, in this secret passageway, the artistry of the stone was notable, and the walls were etched to resemble faux bricks.

Moreover, Tycho could see—despite what the legate had said—that they were not ascending toward the city, but going downwards into the earth. Somehow, they had been fed inaccurate information, and that made Tycho all the more apprehensive, all the more nervous.

Yet eventually the passageway stopped. There was a trapdoor abovehead, and—again in contrast to the reports they'd received—no guard posted below it.

"Now," Tycho whispered, "we succeed, or we meet the gods."

He drew his sword once again out of its scabbard. He layered a hooded cloak over his body as Aulus did the same.  He kissed the cold metal of the blade. He said "Gods give me luck."

And then with a hard thrust, he pushed open the trapdoor.

Darkness was abovehead.

~

When Aulus emerged with his torch, the shadows of the room were dispersed. There were no Ugars in sight, no sign of any kind of life. It was a stone chamber, faced with yellow brick, and in the far corner were barrels and crates of wood, piles of silver and steel objects, and hanging from the ceiling a fur talisman of the Ugars' god Belpheor.

But Aulus and Tycho were safe in one piece, and what's more, they had altogether avoided detection.

The guards at the far end of the passageway had been slain silently.

And two Imperial spies had made it into the heart of the city.

Tycho uttered a prayer of thanksgiving. Then he crouched down.

He tried to catch his breath.

In his day, he had seen many battles, many daring adventures, many times he wondered how on earth he could make it. He had seen armies much larger than the Imperial legion crash and somehow be routed in the midst of war.

His body bore many wounds, many scars from swords that had cut or war-clubs that had bashed him.

It was a wonder he had survived to forty. And yet, his time was not done, no, it was not done.

A task more difficult than any he'd embarked upon was facing him. Like a sword hovering above his head, this mission threatened at any time to go awry, and there were many chances, many opportunities for everything to go horribly wrong.

But for now he could catch his breath; for now he could kneel here and take in the air. For now he could relax, breathe, thank the gods for his lot.

There was a clatter outside… approaching footsteps.

Panic seized Tycho; a look of horror was on Aulus' face. Tycho rushed into the corner and his behind a table. Aulus knelt behind a statue.

The room was dark… it was dark… it would hide him, yes, it would hide Tycho… that was what he told himself.

The door swung open.

A figure was there, an Ugar in a silken purple robe.

The robe was hemmed with red.

On the Ugar's head was a mitre sparkling with crystals.

Two others were behind him, a woman and a man, both young, dressed in plain gray robes.

*A priest,* Tycho thought, and two acolytes.

The Ugars began to speak to each other in their own tongue.

Tycho held his breath. He looked at Aulus and saw that he had done the same.

The Ugar was rummaging through something, a cabinet he realized. The lights of the hall glinted on a key, which the priest put into his pocket.

The Ugar said something; the acolytes scurried away, out of the room, out on ahead.

The priest paused and looked about.

But the room was dark, and the shadows hid Tycho well.

The priest turned and began to walk down the hallway.

And Tycho emerged from the darkness, thanking the gods once more that he was alive, thanking the gods that he could live to see another day.

For now at least… the day was almost done, but the night was still ahead.

Tycho kissed the flat of his blade once more, feeling the cold of the metal on his lips.

This sword had seen much; she had felled many enemies. And she did not have a name.

A standard Imperial issue, she was, made of the finest steel. His old sword had broken; this one had served him now for two years.

Aulus was standing there, just inches from him.

Light from lamps was glowing dimly from down the hall.

Tycho made a signal of two fingers and Aulus nodded wordlessly.

Half-crouching, half-walking, Tycho crept down the hall, half walking, half kneeling.

He knew they were not secure until they left the building and got into the streets. Only then would they become indistinguishable from the Ugars.

The report they'd been given said the passageway ended in the center of the city, but like much of the report it was wrong.

And as Tycho crept through the corridor he could not help but notice the artistry of the walls, how every brick was perfectly fitted in place, how the floors had no sign of chipping or filth. They were in a place of wealth, a place of richness.

~

They plunged through an open door, and found themselves in a vast space. Crowds of people were packed here, women and children, and for that reason Tycho withdrew and waited a moment.

His heart was pounding in his chest.

He recognized the makeup of this place, a crude subterranean keep. The roof was so high it seemed impossible; it was like the vault of the stars but without ornament or decoration.

And a statue of the Ugars' god Belpheor lay in the center

of the room, a hideous thing that dwarfed the people that surrounded it.

Tycho found his heart began to race at the sight of it, at the bull-like head, the naked human body sitting knees crossed, the eyes that seemed to look deep into you.

He was pausing at the threshold. The noise of the combined crowds was enough to mask him; no one had taken note.

He could sense Aulus behind him.

He saw now where they were, but he was more uneasy than ever.

He did not know how to get out. Sometimes, the best way was to roll the die and push ahead.

And so he did, walking out into the open without any sign of fear, his Imperial sword discreetly within its sheath.

He walked in the open through the great chamber, avoiding a glance at the hideous statue, pushing on and on. The women, children and guards did not take note; they continued to sit there silently.

And soon enough Tycho was out of the keep altogether, in the open air, behind enemy lines.

~

Night had fallen over Eioli, the chief city of the Ugars. The stars were bright points against a black canvas and wispy silvery clouds veiled the moon.

And in the city of wonders they were, a city rarely glimpsed by Imperial eyes.

Among its ruins many buildings remained, flat-roofed structures which lined the street and some so tall they leaned into it.

Tycho turned and looked back; there was a shadow against the backdrop of the moon, a many-storied temple reaching to the heavens.

There was so very much to learn.

# Chapter Eight

*Publius Allius Corvus, Legionary*

They were all together, the four members of the Corvus family.

Gathered in Flavia's house in harbor district, they were together; yes, they were together and none of them were apart.

When was the last time it was so?

The sunlight was glinting in through the great window, opening up a vast view of the harbor. The dawn was gold and pink against the sea.

The funeral was today.

But fear had replaced Publius' grief. In the night he had been tormented by dreams he could not remember, and then… then… that creature outside his window was still lurking about somewhere, surely—that was if it were not a dream in and of itself.

Publius tried to focus on the moment: his last day in the city before he returned to Eioli. Would it be the last gathering of the House Corvus? Only time would tell.

"What is Haroon like?" asked Marcella.

She had always been to the point, but Marcus—withered and clearly lacking something—was not likely to give a good answer.

Publius could tell he felt ashamed in the presence of his siblings. After the life he had been living, he seemed to have grown unhealthy; he was thin, and parts of his body were almost skeletal, just skin and bones. But the most haunting feature were his eyes, eyes which had turned a reddish color.

"Haroon," Marcus said. "The Red City… my downfall. I do not think I will go back there. I do not think I can afford to."

Marcus had brought along something curious; in his time

in that great city of the east, he had taken up smoking and now the odor hung heavy over the house. But what was more curious was the substance he put in his pipe, coarse red sand-like grains, the color of blood, which he called "spice." It clearly affected him, and last night, after he had let the vapors enter his body, he had staggered about and spoken nonsense; he had seen visions, claiming the presence of another, claiming to see spirits all over the house. The substance he called "spice" seemed to have done him in, and thrice he had asked Publius for money—money he could not afford to give.

Publius wondered what had happened. He had witnessed his father give away the family business to the favored son; he had, at least then, nursed resentments and envies. But seeing his brother now made him realize how wrong he had been.

He had spent his money on things that destroyed him; and look at him now.

Flavia touched Marcus' hand. "Well," she said, "you are with us now. You do not have to worry."

Publius knew her words were empty. There were always things to worry about, always danger. At any moment one's life could take a turn for the worse; at any moment one could die.

He had seen it for himself outside his window; a creature, half-phantom, half-ghul, just inches from him.

Whatever it was had sought him out; whatever it was was hunting him.

He had not told his sisters or brother for fear of scaring them. He wondered if he should let them know; but he did not know if he would be believed. How many times had Marcus given him that sidelong look, that glance of superiority? But Marcus was different now.

He was worn down, and in his eyes there was sadness.

"Father," Flavia said, "was a good man."

Caius Corvus, born in Mud Bottom, was the richest man

on Seafarer's Way. He had provided for all of them.

But Publius had always felt he was second best, the least favored of the children. Caius Corvus had always doted on Marcus.

"He was," he said, and at the thought of having lost him tears appeared anew, and Publius began to cry.

At his tears Flavia began to cry, then Marcella. Demetrius and Marcus remained stoic, stone-faced, without a hint of emotion.

~

They rose; they prepared. They dressed in solemn black. A coach was waiting outside. Their father was to be honored, and they were all to be there.

# Chapter Nine

*Constantius Pello, Speaker in Absentia*

The morning light was shining through the Council House's Oculus.

Constantius was standing there, preparing for the Council's convening, and as the sunlight covered him he felt like a messenger of the gods, cloaked in light, wreathed in blessing.

It had assembled, the people's council, representing the city's thirty wards.

They were seated on benches in this circular room, this room had seen so much history, so many consequential decisions. It was a room that held sway over an entire nation, whose pronouncements and laws impacted the whole peninsula.

*"Numera!"* Constantius said out of respect for the lawful Speaker Agatho.

The Legis strode forward and began to count; twenty-five were here and the Council could proceed.

Constantius had a law to pass, a law whose true purpose he did not understand, but one he was keen to benefit from.

The builders had formed a company of sorts, and whatever their purposes for their construction Constantius had made sure not to ask.

There was no payment for the position of councilor; only those already rich were expected to assume it. Moneys were made in other ways but by law bribes such as what Constantius expected were illegal.

"I move," said Lucius Saius, the blond-haired councilor from East Fork, "that the first order of business be the disappearance of our Marshal of the Guard."

"I do not object," Constantius said. There was still time to propose his law.

And indeed the vanishing of the Marshal of the Guard had raised questions. He was gone, and now there was no suitable candidate to replace him.

Tidus Sulpicius Varro, a military man who had been universally well regarded, had been assigned to guard the emperor before his murder.

Constantius drew back to the shadows of the room as Saius stepped downward to begin his speech.

"Tidus Sulpicius Varro," Saius said. "Who remembers his name? Who recalls his valor in the Battle of Marmuk? Who recalls his patriotism, his love of country?

"And now it seems this body has abandoned him.

"Where we turned up every corner, looked in every hidden room, and scoured the entire city for Julia Seánus, we have not expended any effort or resource to find the Marshal of the Guard, and now his post is vacant."

His post was vacant because it did not seem urgent during Council rule, but Constantius decided not to bring it up.

"I propose to create a commission," Saius continued, "of able bodied and sure minded men to find Tidus Sulpicius Varro. Some believe he was kidnapped… some believe he was killed?"

"And what," said the oldest member of the Council, Lychicus, striding forward on his cane, "if he disappeared on his own? What if he chose to vanish?"

"Nonsense," Saius said.

Constantius watched from the shadows of the room as the Legis strode forward. It was an obvious violation, one Saius likely knew.

"Out of order," he said. "Begin again." And like that the Legis was back in the background.

"A proposal," Saius said, "for an inquiry. A commission worthy of a veteran of our wars, a commission worthy of someone we all know. Let us find him. Let us do our best to uncover the mystery. Let us find answers."

There was silence for what seemed like a minute.

The Legis walked forth; Saius returned to his bench.

"No objection," the Legis said. "A commission will be formed. This is the last order of the day."

As the clerk furiously scribbled on his parchment, Constantius spoke up at almost a shout: "I have a proposal," he said.

The Legis looked a bit bothered. "I yield the floor."

~

The more he spoke, the more he explained, the more unconvinced the faces of the councilors looked. Stoic they were, the elders of the nation, dozens of gray-haired faces looking down upon him.

Lychicus looked almost angry. And when Constantius finished explaining the proposal, it was Lychicus who spoke first.

"Why," Lychicus said, "are you so insistent on this construction, Signor Speaker?"

He began to descend the steps and Constantius reluctantly withdrew.

"Friends, Imperials, fellow countrymen." The oldest of the Council was now standing in the center of the room with the sunlight from the oculus beaming to his left. "We are engaged in a war with the Ugars. The treasury of the Empire is not unlimited, and I move that we are custodians of our nation's wealth; we cannot waste the money on ourselves, not when our nation's finest are in Ugarit, risking their lives because of us. This idiotic proposal—"

"Objection!" Constantius said, and there was more wrath in his voice than he wanted to let slip. "Insulting a member of the body…"

He said those words through gritted teeth.

But the Legis lifted a hand. "Denied… the insult was to your proposal. The speaker must yield the floor."

And so, one after another, the councilors of the Imperial government strode forth, condemning the law.

Worst of all were their suspicious looks.

In the end, the vote was fifteen to ten, an abject failure.

Constantius had failed his co-conspirators and he left the chambers fearful of what would come next.

# Chapter Ten

*Varius Tycho, Legionary*

Tycho had slept little over the prior night.

He and Aulus, hidden behind barrels on a quiet Eioli street, had managed to avoid detection. The stars had passed them by in their nightly procession and now Tycho—barely able to stay awake—was watching the city stir to life.

Tycho and Aulus were a little taller than most Ugars, and so it would be difficult to blend in. But they were here on a mission, a mission sanctioned by the Empire. They had both been on many dangerous quests before, ones that had posed serious risks to their lives.

Several times Tycho had come within an inch of death where, if his body were positioned just slightly off he would have perished—just like many of his brothers-in-arms had.

Tycho stood up and, drawing his hooded cloak about him, walked onward down the street. Aulus followed him a step behind.

~

The morning sun was shining and above the noise of carriages, horses and chatter, the sound of a drum and cymbal was rising.

As Tycho walked, the Ugars did not seem to take note, though he was often half again their size.

The streets were crowded, the buildings flat roofed. Every street was paved with gold stones. And in the air everywhere was the scent of spice and the feeling of mystery and magic.

The street opened up into a city square; there, in the center of it, was a great statue.

Hideous it was, the form of their god Belpheor. It was bronze and beneath its metallic hands was a great fire that was raging.

The drummers were beside it, tapping the drums with their hands, and another musician making use of a cymbal.

Aulus was headed toward the fire but Tycho put a hand on his shoulder. "Wait," Tycho whispered, and as they turned he could sense the mood in the crowd change.

With them behind his back he heard a shout, "You there! Stop!"

Tycho could not help but turn; the people in the market square were all looking at him.

So many faces, so many faces in the crowd. And Tycho felt his hand going to his sword.

"Unveil your hood!" the same voice cried and out of the sea of people a figure emerged, a tall Ugar, dark-skinned, dark-eyed, with a crystal hat on his head and silk robes of purple and gold. His dark eyes were twinkling, and a smile was growing on his face.

Tycho lowered his hood. He would face this danger as he had faced all dangers before, and he would emerge victorious.

From his sheath he drew his sword. Openly he stared at the priest.

He looked at the bronze statue and the fire beneath its hands, and he wondered if the rumors were true, the legends that had spread among the people of Imperial City, the myths he had always chalked up to defamation and slander. Would someone be so cruel as to sacrifice a human?

He glared at the priest openly. "I come from the Empire," he said, "and I intend to see this city burned to the ground."

There was an uproar in the crowd, angry shouts and sidelong hisses.

The priest's expression changed from jubilation to indignation.

Tycho turned and ran.

~

Aulus was following him as he sprinted through the streets.

Tycho cast aside obstacles furiously—kegs and barrels, crates and even bystanders. He was tracing his way back to where he had come from, to the tunnel from which he had emerged.

Ugar soldiers appeared before him, blocking his path. He swiped with his sword; steel met steel and then he plunged his blade through the soldier's heart.

Another kill; another death, and Tycho was not happy about it.

He struck the other soldier; steel met steel. He struck again; steel met steel again. He kicked the soldier with his boot and he fell onto his back. He finished the job with his sword, and blood spurted, spraying him in the face.

Tycho turned back; he looked. Aulus was nowhere in sight.

Aulus was an essential part of this aborted mission. In such circumstances, Imperial law demanded Tycho save himself.

He had known Aulus only a few hours, but he was still a brother.

He kissed his blade and motioned in the wind. "Godspeed, Aulus. I hope you make it."

And then he turned and ran, bolting through the streets, overturning carts, pushing Ugars aside. He sprinted as fast as he could, and as he was running down the way he saw Aulus sprinting as well.

His brother was alive.

And then together they ran; together they bolted, through the streets, and the Ugars did not stand a chance.

Behind them they were, and ahead of them, but they ran as fast as their legs would carry them.

And then they entered the donjon-keep, bearing swords together.

They turned down the way, through the open door, running, running, running. The gods were with them and the nation's fate was on their shoulders.

# Chapter Eleven

*Publius Allius Corvus, Legionary*

The temple of Hieronus lay on the edge of the Imperial City ward known as Mud Bottom.

It was shaped, like all Hieronian temples, like a crude hammer. Its windows were of blue glass and its green roof contrasted sharply with the gray stone it was composed of.

It was the temple where Father prayed; it was the temple he had taken his children to on feast days and high holy days. It was the temple where Publius and his siblings would pay their respects. It was the temple where he would finally be bidden goodbye.

~

Within, benches faced the altar. Before the altar was a coffin and standing there was a priest of Hieronus.

Hieronus was the god of justice. He was the god of just war. He was the god that Caius Corvus, and the Corvus family in general, paid their most respects to.

Publius did not have a preference. But it was here, in these stone walls, where his childhood had been forged, where he had met so many children, where he had grown up, had witnessed weddings and funerals. In a sense, it was where he had been made.

He was somber as he walked to the front of the benches. His father was lying there in a gentle repose, though all the best undertakers could not make him what he was. What lay there was a corpse, a thing, not his father in any sense, a body without a soul. And at the sight of it tears began to well up.

Publius had so many regrets. He turned to see only a few people scattered throughout the temple. So few had come to honor him. But Publius would. Though he had given the family business to his brother, though he had given Marcus all his affection, Publius would not hold it against him. No, he would not. He was a man, self-sufficient. He was a man with his own life, his own path.

Around the corpse's neck was a medallion, a hammer of Hieronus that he had always worn.

"I will take this," he said, and the priest made no objection.

From his father's body he took the hammer. He would wear it around his neck like his father had. All day and all night it would be with him, a memory of his father, a reminder of the gods in heaven.

He laid it over himself. He turned to see Flavia and the others, none with disapproving glances.

"Father," he said, turning once again to the body—the shell of flesh which was not him—and said, "I miss you."

# Chapter Twelve

*Varius Tycho, Legionary*

Tycho and Aulus had broken through the breaches. Into the heart of the donjon-keep they had fled, but as they ran—pursued by hundreds of Ugars—it dawned on Tycho that he did not know where he was going, that he did not know where the tunnel began, and how he would get out.

And so he ran, he simply ran, through the corridors, past statues and ossuaries, past urns and hidden chambers and storehouses beneath the earth.

He stopped at a dead end, before an open door. Beyond the door was a great chamber and there—plain to the eye—was glittering gold, a mound bigger than any he had ever seen.

It was like a mountain was Eioli's gold, in a chamber the size of entire villages, piled high from the floor to the ceiling. Coins and jeweled goblets were there, necklaces twinkling with diamonds and hills and hills of gold bars. Such wealth was impossible to imagine, and Tycho could not help but admit a twinge of lust at the sight of it.

It was like the size of the Imperial palace, the room, so vast you could fit a small city in it.

And Tycho stood there agape, for a moment unaware that the Ugars were pursuing, or uncaring.

He could not imagine that there was this much gold in the world, let alone in a city.

Twinkling it was, mountains of coins.

Aulus shouted, and his attention turned again.

The Ugars had cornered them.

But Tycho brandished his sword. "Aulus!" he said as he charged forth. "Record what you have seen…"

The Ugars had boxed them in but Tycho charged forward; spear against sword, shield against sword it was. He cut an Ugar down and the others began to view him timidly; though he was outnumbered and outflanked he continued to press, and he began to make way.

"Finished!" Aulus said and Tycho looked back; Aulus was sliding his roll of parchment into his cloak.

Then he drew his sword, and the shield which he had hidden, and charged headlong, and the Ugars—though wildly outnumbering them—broke rank.

They charged forth and the Ugars fell back; they cut their way through. The gods were with them and they found the tunnel. The gods were with them and they were making their way out.

# Chapter Thirteen

*Constantius Pello, Speaker in Absentia*

Night was setting in. The moon was rising above the city. Constantius was standing on the sky bridge, above the dull glow of the buildings.

The sting of failure was all about him, the failure of the passage of the law.

And now he had gotten himself into trouble, for the scheme itself was illegal, and he did not trust the shady characters he had gotten into business with. Indeed, he wondered what their reaction would be to failure. He wondered if they would punish him, or worse, if his secret would get out.

It was time to get home. His business for the day and night were done, and yet he lingered.

There was fear in his heart, fear bubbling up, fear that went beyond just the failures of the day. He recalled Gray Hood— whatever his true name was—and that he was only the face of an organization which did not say its name. What had he gotten himself into? He had placed himself at the center of a crime, and now, Gray Hood's superiors knew his name and knew what he would be willing to do for coin.

He turned.

A creature was there, pale white—no, a woman, no, a thing.

She was crouched over and her skin was bloodless. Her eyes were like black marbles and her fingernails—dead and dark— were overgrown.

Constantius hadn't a moment to react before she was lunging, before she was tackling him to the ground.

Such eyes he had never seen, pitch black yet full of malice and wrath. Her teeth were bright white, but as she wrestled him to the ground his last thought was of the book he had read, the entry he had laughed at, the legend of the Strig.

The last thing he felt was his energy draining away. His will and his desire to live evaporated into the night, until he was gone from the world.

# Interlude I

The Red Lord was filled with anger.

His servants had tried mightily to find the girl, or so they claimed, but they had come back empty-handed.

The girl had claimed to be one of them. But she was not.

Her very name was a symbol of the Empire which the Red Lord hated. She exemplified it; she exuded the nation from her very being.

The woman at the Red Lord's right hand had changed her, thinking it worse than death.

But it was not. For there was still a chance for her, still a slight sliver of hope.

# Chapter Fourteen

*Publius Allius Corvus*

It was late when they returned from the cemetery.

Publius' father had been buried in the Corvus family plot far outside the city bounds.

And now the moon was glowing over the city, and the stars were bright pinpoints of light.

Publius was walking with Flavia, Marcella, Demetrius and Marcus, and on this walk he had heard the first laugh from Marcus since he'd gotten home.

They were almost to Mud Bottom. The lights of the Council House and the Imperial Palace were in the distance. The streets were dark. Publius did not want to leave this place of love, but tomorrow duty called. Tomorrow, he would return to Eioli. He would return still full of sorrow, but he would fight with all his might. He had taken an oath, and honorable men took oaths seriously.

A shadow was approaching, crouching yet walking. Flavia screamed, and amid the silence of the night a noise arose, a low growl like that of an angry dog.

It was a creature, no a woman, yes a creature—a humanoid form… a bent over, crouching form. Two black eyes stared at them.

Demetrius brandished his dagger.

They were on a lonely road, and no members of the urban cohorts were posted nearby.

Publius was without his sword.

"Publius," the creature said, the word rising above the growl. "Publius!"

It dawned on him in that moment that he and the creature had met before, that this creature growling and bent over had been outside his bedroom window.

Her eyes were black and solid, yet though featureless they seemed angry.

She lunged; Publius did not know what to do, but asking the gods' aid he removed the Hieronus hammer from his neck and begged for their deliverance.

At the sight of the symbol the creature was backing away; no longer were her marble black eyes full of wrath but instead full of fear.

"What is it?" Flavia screamed, and Marcella gasped.

Clearly, they'd seen nothing like it.

Nor had Publius until days ago.

The creature there was gangly, but retained a human form. She—or it—had wisps of white hair that fell to her back and overall she smelled of death, like a corpse that had been sitting out in the sun.

What was it? What could it be?

"Publius!" the creature said, and this time it was a screech; this time it was like the sound of a dying thing, a wounded animal harried by the hunter's arrow.

"Publius!" she wailed but if she was trying to gain sympathy Publius had none.

He drew nearer her, holding the holy symbol out, projecting it before her. And as he drew near, she began to change; the wispy white hairs began to change to blonde, her black eyes began to acquire white edges.

"Publius," she said, a desperate cry, and this time he recognized her voice. "Publius… help me…"

She turned and fled, darting down an alleyway.

Julia it was… Julia… and she had been changed.

# Chapter Fifteen

*Publius Allius Corvus, Legionary*

The nightmare of what Publius had seen bothered him only in the evening and when he bade his siblings good night and went to sleep, his sleep was peaceful.

For the first night since he'd left Eioli, he was at rest, but when morning came and the sun shone, it dawned on him that Julia—whatever had happened—was still there. He did not fully understand what had happened to her, but could she be helped?

As expected, in the light of dawn the government official was standing there, garbed head to toe in a black hood.

The coach was waiting there and three horses were pulling it.

The door swung open; Flavia came out, weeping. "Goodbye, brother. Goodbye… I love you."

"I love you, too," Publius said, and only then did he realize this could be the last time they'd meet, the last time they'd see each other. Eioli was well fortified and the Ugars were fierce when cornered.

Marcus came out too, still dressed in his bedclothes.

"I hope to see you soon, brother," he said, and in turn Publius embraced him.

"And I as well," Publius answered.

But it was time to go; the time had come.

His eyes were welling with tears as he hopped in the coach. *Goodbye to Father. Goodbye to my brother, and my sisters.*

~

The coach was rattling through the streets and Publius was

looking out the slit-like windows. The streets were crowded, as they always were in Imperial City on sunny autumn days.

He watched as the coach turned down several thoroughfares and avenues.

He watched as the buildings went by.

He was full of thought and pondering.

Eventually the street gave way to the grandeur of Imperial Square, the vast plaza where the western and northern roads met.

Publius thought of Eioli. He thought of the task ahead of him. He wondered if the Empire could succeed, but above all he wondered if the Empire should succeed.

He had never been tested in battle; he had only been trained, but he had wielded the sword with the best of them. Yet what would he do on the front lines, face to face with the enemy, shields locked man to man, pressing forward, laying siege to the city's walls?

The coach came to a crashing halt. Screams rang out, wild high-pitched screams. The horses of the coach shrieked and neighed wildly.

~

Publius opened the door and fell out of the coach, sword in hand, dizzy with movement.

Pandemonium had erupted in Imperial Square.

Right before him a woman was lying on the ground, blood spurting from her cut throat like a fountain.

And locked in this nightmare, this nightmare he did not want to believe was real, Publius could feel his heart pounding. His head was swimming as if viscous fluid were swirling inside.

Was it real?

Yes, he guessed it was... bodies on the street, lying bleeding.

In the distance, red-cloaked figures were running away, and members of the urban cohorts were pursuing them.

He turned; the horses pulling the coach had their throats cut and were slumped in their reins.

The government official who'd been driving it was lying on the stones of Imperial Square bleeding.

There was a wild scream, lighting up the autumn day.

A woman was charging him, garbed in a red cloak, eyes mad with fury.

How could such horror occur on such a beautiful autumn day?

Publius was still staggered when the woman's knife pierced him, but he quickly awoke from his stupor.

Though still reeling, though still unable to comprehend such carnage and why, why, why it had occurred, he drew his sword.

It was dishonorable to slay a woman, but she would kill him, and her eyes were dark and evil, like one possessed.

He slashed with his sword and cut her open; she fell screaming to the ground, indignant—it seemed—that he had dared to defend himself.

What had happened?

What on earth had happened?

And why had it occurred on such a beautiful autumn day?

Trumpets were sounding, a succession of trumpets.

Cavalry from the urban cohorts were galloping in. One on a horse was riding towards Publius, one on a horse, girt in armor, with a bright helm on his head and a red crest that flowed from it.

"You… are you all right?" he shouted.

"Yes," Publius lied. "Yes… yes I am."

# Part Two

# Chapter Sixteen

*Publius Allius Corvus, Legionary*

"What happened?" the tribune said, questioning Publius in a dark room. "What do you remember?"

"Red…" Publius said.

"Blood?" the tribune continued.

"No," Publius said, "red clothing. They were all wearing red."

The tribune had brought a stunned Publius to a building in the shadow of the Imperial Palace.

He was still reeling, still unable to believe what he had seen.

And as he sat there in the light of the windows and the dull illumination of the lamps he realized he was struggling to come to terms with it, struggling even to remember.

Just what had happened?

The images were difficult to get out of his head—the people, cut down by knives and lying in various states of deterioration; the once-pristine stones of Imperial Square stained with blood and viscera.

He had not seen such carnage before in his life, and he was still unsettled, still reeling.

"I was headed back to my duties… to Eioli," Publius said. "Say, am I still headed back? When do I go?"

"Do not worry about that," the tribune answered. "Your journey has been suspended… for now.

"Tell me, Publius Corvus… did you recognize anyone? Did you see anyone you knew among the assassins? Members of the military?"

Publius did not want to think a member of the legion would turn his sword on the people of Imperial City, but then he did not know such evil existed; he was still haunted by the woman's eyes, so black and so full of bloodlust, such empty pits that seemed to lead into the abyss.

"No," Publius said, "I recognized no one."

Memories were returning, memories he had blocked out.

"But…" he said. "On the way there… I might have seen something. I—"

"What did you see?" the tribune pressed him.

"On one of the roads to Imperial Square, I thought I saw…. I thought…" He paused, not knowing how to explain. "Let me show you."

~

Imperial Square was empty now; city workers were cleaning up the blood and removing the bodies. It was eerie to see it like this, when it was such a place of activity before, where noise there was and lights, and colors. Now it was silent, and that silence was eating at Publius.

He tried to recall the street that the coach was rattling through. Many streets connected to Imperial Square, not just the main thoroughfare.

But with the tribune and a coterie of legionaries behind him, Publius made his way to the edge and eventually found it, a narrow street called "King's Way."

The entryway to Imperial Square had been blocked off, now, by fencing, so Publius hopped over it. He pushed through the light crowds of people with the tribune behind him.

On the wall of a tavern he found it: a handprint in red ink whose lively color had faded in the sunlight.

"Here," Publius said. "It did not strike me as odd when I saw it. But after what happened, I remembered…   I… there's something about it.

"And there were people gathered near it, talking to each other. Strange people."

The handprint was stylized, almost a symbol in its contours. It had to have greater meaning but what meaning Publius couldn't imagine.

He turned to the tribune, who appeared unimpressed. He was looking somberly at the handprint, but there was no emotion to his eyes.

Clearly whatever he had seen did not make a connection in the tribune's mind, but when Publius turned to look at the marking once more it seemed all the more odd, so symbolic, so—seemingly—full of meaning, each finger stylized in a particular way. It was not made by a human hand but it had been painted on the walls of the tavern.

"This," the tribune said, "is what you saw?"

Publius nodded.

~

In the ensuing days, the event acquired many names: "The Day of the Knives," "the Great Massacre," even—inexplicably—the "Red Dawn."

Publius, whom the tribune said was the only living witness, was made to stay in Imperial City, though he longed to go, though he longed to fight in Eioli, or be anywhere away from here.

# Chapter Seventeen

*Varius Tycho, Legionary*

The day after Tycho and Aulus escaped, just barely emerging from Eioli alive, they broke bread together and drank as much wine as the legions would allow.

The report had been made; Aulus' observations had been recorded.

In the afternoon they would meet with the Grand Legate Lornodoris and explain what they had seen.

And what they had seen still lingered with Tycho. As he sipped the wine on the outskirts of camp, still exhausted, still reeling, he found he could not forget the image of that gold, of mountains of coins so high he could not imagine such wealth existing in all the world.

Yes it lingered. He had no idea the city of Eioli was so rich. Centuries it had existed, millennia, the queen of Ugarit, collecting taxes and engaging in commerce from all corners of the world. Proud she had sat by the shores of the sea, and when the Imperials arrived she had hated them. Now she resisted… but Tycho and Aulus had seen what she hid, what she had tried so mightily to keep safe. Wealth untold lay in her donjon-keep, wealth far beyond what anyone could have imagined.

Pillaging was never the official policy of the Imperial government; but for such a sum it would be tempting. For such a sum, who could resist stretching the bounds of the law?

The sun was beating hot. The tents of the camp were to their left; Eioli's dark walls were ahead, and so too were the legions encamped around, the legions which—for weeks now—had lain silent, not attacking on the orders of their Grand Legate.

Yet if they intended to starve the Ugars out, Tycho had seen no signs of strain despite the ruins of buildings and the remnants of the siege. Eioli was rich; she was the Queen of Ugarit, and no doubt her storehouses were full, packed each year with grain from every fruitful harvest.

"Well done, I'd say," Tycho told Aulus.

Aulus looked up from his bread. He took a sip of his wine. "And a well-deserved meal."

Tycho nodded his approval.

~

The grand legate's tent was not normally the largest of them all. Out of humility, a grand legate would often have no special accommodations.

Not so with this grand legate, Agatho Lornodoris.

It was palatial, in fact, and on the floor of the tent—forming makeshift carpets—were bear skins and the pelts of wolves and deer. The air was warm, stuffy even, and in the thickness of it there was the scent of flavored candles—pine resin, it smelled like.

Two guards were posted at the threshold of the inner chamber.

To live so well, Tycho thought, was an insult to Lornodoris' men and a mark against his character. He had heard that this Lornodoris fellow was an August, the Speaker of the Council even, and so this was his first foray into the military. Still, he should know. Still, he should have possessed the character.

Tycho slid his sword into its sheath and then buckled it to his belt. Aulus followed suit.

Perhaps, Lornodoris did not deserve respect; but the office did.

From the tent-fold of the inner chamber a man came walking out, garbed in rich gray. "The Legate will hear you now."

Lornodoris was a tall man, taller even than Tycho.

And he was old, yes, he was old. Tycho had heard he was pushing seventy but this man was decrepit, and his face was thickly wrinkled. His eyes were gray and pale, and one had a bloodshot character to it.

Though he was tall, he seemed small; he seemed weary and tired.

And what's more, there were two spots near either eyebrow, wounds that had not yet healed.

"Soldiers," he said. "What do you have for me?"

At his words he began to cough, and for several moments that was all he did, hacking and wheezing. Then, in silence and embarrassment, he looked at the two men before him in expectation.

Aulus stepped forward with the parchment scroll. "Signor Legate," he said simply. "A report for your eyes, and the eyes of the Council."

Lornodoris took the parchment and opened it, reading it only cursorily. His eyes turned to Aulus. "Tell me," he said, "in your own words, what you saw."

"Riches beyond measure," Aulus said. "A chamber in the inner keep, a chamber the size of the entire Imperial Palace back home, deep beneath the earth. It was filled, almost to the ceiling, with gold."

Yet if this tale of riches intrigued Lornodoris, he did not show it; he did not show it at all.

His glassy eyes showed no sign of interest, no spark of intrigue.

"Gold, you say," Lornodoris began. "According to our laws, banditry is not cause for a just war."

Tycho was no lawyer, but he knew a little. "Not a cause," Tycho said, "but even our own laws do not prohibit nature. To the victor go the spoils. If we—according to the laws of just war—conquer Eioli, then that gold could be ours."

Lornodoris was looking at them sourly now.

"Gold," he muttered. "Is that what our nation is, now? Bandits and brigands?"

He withdrew and shadow seemed to linger all about him.

"Gold, gold," Lornodoris said. "Is that what you think this is about? Is that what you think is it at stake? Gold? Just gold, Varius Tycho? Just gold, Aulus Meridius?"

Now he seemed afraid.

But he spoke again, and this time there was a note of confidence in his voice, almost command: "I will send your report to the Imperial Council. You have done your duties. You have completed the task that the nation assigned to you. You have honored your oath."

He said it as if he were not personally pleased.

But Tycho would take it; every word he'd said was true. All he had done was for the nation; all he had done was for his oath. He had completed his task honorably."

"Go," Lornodoris said, "report to your centurions. You will hear from me soon."

Were they about to commence the siege? Tycho supposed he would have to wait.

# Chapter Eighteen

*Vello Lychicus, Councilor*

Lychicus had witnessed so much in his seventy-five years, twenty of which had been spent in the Empire's most August chamber.

But standing in the light of the sun, on the Sky Bridge, he realized nothing compared to this horror.

It was without explanation, the corpse before him, the Speaker in Absentia Constantius.

He was shriveled and a shade of blue; his body had shrunken in size and the robe now looked so big on him it was like a blanket.

Worst of all was the expression on his face, an expression of pure terror, like one who had stared into the abyss.

"What is this?" Lychicus said.

Four other councilors were with him, four other councilors who had come here for various morning duties.

The Council had not been pledged to be in session.

Lychicus and the four others had stumbled upon Constantius' corpse.

They were staring in stunned silence. In the end it was Majorius, the councilor from Villa Fort, that spoke first.

"It seems…" Majorius began. "I… I don't know."

He stooped down on his old knees, brushed the withered skin of Constantius' hand with his own.

"He is as dry as a mummy," Majorius said.

It was a pointed thing to say. Mummification was a barbarian custom that the Khazidees followed; believing that a body must survive, intact, until the coming of the gods, to achieve eternal life, they would pick apart organs and ensure it would never rot.

And yet he spoke truth; Constantius resembled a fresh mummy, one which had been recently worked on.

The skin was pulled tight across the bones, and though there was a scent of death he was not rotting in the ways bodies normally did. There was no bloating, no greenish tint, just a look of horror.

"But what," Majorius continued, "what would explain that… that… he is shrunken?"

"We shall call a physician," Lychicus said. "And make preparations for a funeral… he must receive full state honors."

The Lychicus family had been in the Imperial annals for generations. At the time of the Unification, they had belonged to the Formusus tribe. They had seen the Empire through its perils; they had seen the Empire as it began to rise.

Constantius was of the Pello family, a family that was of little note, but which belonged to the August class. He deserved the Council's respect, and the Council's formal honor.

"Call the Legis," said Lychicus. "The Council convenes this morning."

~

Bells were rung, bells in towers throughout Imperial City, bells of a certain timbre and a certain rhythm. Those bells summoned the Imperial government to order, and councilors— even if not obligated—were expected to respond, to set their work down and meet in the Council Chamber's majestic halls.

Lychicus took his seat and waited, and as the morning drew on, he began to grow impatient.

It was three hours after dawn when the first of the councilors emerged. One by one they trickled in, the members of the Empire's most revered body.

The Legis waited dressed in his pseudo military uniform; the clerk had sat before his table, and his book was already open.

Lychicus strode forward, leaning on his cane. After the Speaker in Absentia he was the Councilor who had served the longest, and so—in these strange and desperate times—he would fill their functions.

He counted twenty-seven seated, almost a full roster.

"I have summoned the Council," Lychicus said. "Let the Legis count. *Numera!*"

But the Legis did not begin the roll. Instead, he walked up and beckoned Lychicus to step aside.

Lychicus realized the Legis was holding a sheet of parchment in his hand, a parchment of law.

And so Lychicus obeyed; he revered custom and honored tradition.

"Councilors," Lychicus said, "according to the ancient law… according to the customs passed down by our ancestors… members of the Council, Imperials all. The Speaker is absent; his replacement has been slain.

"And so this Council may not legally convene until an emperor is named.

"An emperor must be named. It is according to our law. The White Throne cannot sit vacant.

"Make haste in your choice, Councilors, but do your diligence…"

# Chapter Nineteen

*Publius Allius Corvus, Legionary*

The longer he spent in this building, which he'd learned was called Fort Mettius, the more he was able to rest; the more he was able to rest, the more he was able to come to terms with what had happened, and the more he remembered.

And so, he was lingering in the main hall, with legionaries and centurions from the urban cohorts going this way in that.

He recalled at that moment a little more information, that, as his coach was wheeling his way through Imperial Square, he had seen something—no, he had seen someone.

Yes, at the perimeter of the square, so distant he could barely make him out, as business went on in Imperial Square, he was lingering… a man in military dress but with a red cloak about his shoulders, wearing not a helmet but a wreath of pine cones and of ivy.

He stood up from his seat.

In his time in Fort Mettius, dazed and disoriented, he had learned the name of the tribune, Gnaius. Friendship was too strong a term, but Publius had learned to trust him in a world where trust was lacking, in a world where so few deserved it.

And more he remembered… more… yes, he would tell Gnaius everything.

~

"A man in military garb?" Gnaius said.

The light was filtering in through the windows. The autumn morning would be beautiful and full of promise if it were not stained with memories. The Massacre of 210 Y.E. would be remembered forever in history, Publius guessed, and still they did not know the culprits.

"Military garb?" Publius answered. "No… but he was wearing a breastplate. And there was an eagle insignia on it. An eagle… like…"

Gnaius proffered a tablet of slate and a chalk pen.

Publius got to work. The eagle was stylized, like most Imperial heraldry, but it was stylized in a unique way, with a beak raised up to the heavens and dark black spots for eyes.

Gnaius gazed upon it. "I know you are not a liar, Publius," he said. "But what you've just drawn is the symbol of the Imperial Guard. Perhaps your memory betrays you."

"No," Publius said, "I remember it as clear as day… just before it all happened, just seconds before the knives were pulled out."

Those terrible moments were coming back to him, assassins flinging aside their disguises, bearing cloaks the color of blood, plunging knives into everyone in their sight.

And more memories had returned, worse ones, ones he dared not name to Gnaius. He had heard the coachman being dragged from his seat. He had heard the horses' throats being cut. And like a coward he had remained inside the coach; like a coward he had not done what his oath required.

He had not protected the coachman; he had not defended him. Publius would have died, but now he lived on in shame.

"I'm still… I'm still trying to come to terms with it all."

"I understand," Gnaius replied. "Perhaps, you had best get some rest. See if you can remember anything else."

Publius watched as Gnaius left the room, and, notably, took the tablet of slate with him. Perhaps, he took Publius more seriously than he'd indicated.

~

It was night.

Publius was in his spare quarters.

He knew, any day now, he'd be recalled; he'd be sent back to where he had come, back to the siege of Eioli.

But the horror lingered, the shock of what he had seen, what he was still trying to comprehend.

He did not want to go.

He peered out his window.

From his vantage point, he could see Imperial Square. Life was slowly beginning to return there.

There were lights visible, colored lanterns in various shades of red, green and blue. In the distance he could almost make out the sound of music.

In his youth, he'd been forbidden to go Imperial Square. Those mischievous youths with lenient parents would allow their children to go, but not Caius Corvus—not Caius Corvus, rest his soul. He would not allow his sons to cavort with prostitutes or listen to the bawdy talk of jesters.

Yet even now, in the night, he could see it was less vibrant than before, that it had lost a bit of its life and vivaciousness. There were only a few silhouettes wandering this way and that. The memory of the horror lingered.


The moon was out. Publius guessed it was about midnight.

He did not know why he had awoken, why he had stirred from his slumber.

He looked out the window and the creature was there.

He screamed.

She seemed to be floating, the undead thing, the monstrous being which once had been Julia.

She had followed him; she had somehow climbed up the steep fort walls, or perhaps she had flown… for her index claw was scraping against the glass of the window, but her body was drifting in the air, as if she were swimming in water.

Her black eyes like marbles stared. She smiled, and when she smiled Publius saw fangs.

"Let me in," she cooed. "Let me in, Publius… friend… I won't hurt you."

Publius smiled, touched the window lock, and pretended to give in only a moment before snatching the holy symbol he'd placed near his bed.

She recoiled at the sight of the holy symbol, the hammer of Hieronus forged of silver which his father had always worn around his neck. She floated backward, screaming, and then she fell.

Publius looked down and saw her hit the ground; she darted off like a shadow in the night, fast as a panther.

What had happened to Julia?

If his brothers and sisters hadn't been there with him, seeing her just as he had, Publius would have thought he was suffering from delusions.

But no, Julia was there… Julia had been changed as if by some dark sorcery.

And the longer this all went on, the more he wondered if he could help her… if she could be turned back to her original state.

But that, for now, was beyond his control.

She was now haunting the streets of Imperial City, a ghostlike being hunting those she remembered in her prior life.

But whatever she tried to do in this state, Publius had the holy symbol; he had the protection of the gods.

Could he help her? He did not know. But he knew he was leaving soon. Soon enough, he'd again be on a coach to Eioli. Soon enough, he would be on the front lines of the Empire's wars.

# Chapter Twenty

*Publius Allius Corvus, Legionary*

The morning light was flooding in to the mess hall.

On a table, Publius had a serving of bread. There was a little helping of wine, a watered-down mixture intended only for slaking one's thirst.

And as soon as he tasted the liquid, as soon as the red richness touched his tongue, he thought of Julia.

The incredibleness of it struck him.

As he came to terms with the massacre, with the Day of the Knives, he was also trying to wrestle with something else.

Was it possible for multiple people to suffer from a delusion?

~

The chaplain was in a corner of Fort Mettius.

There, in the shrine, was an altar fronted by pews, and on the altar a length of cloth.

Here, the devout among legionaries would receive spiritual services. It was considered essential to the workings of the army; and the priest was seen as a priest of all the gods, not just one in particular.

The priest was in the corner, tending to the candles. Over his body a green robe was laid. Over his head was a blue hood. He turned and looked at Publius dourly.

"Can I help you, brother?" he said.

Brother. It was a quaint term, a term of respect, a term all followers of the gods were expected to honor.

"Brother," he said. "May I talk to you in private? A word…

I don't want it to get out. I don't understand it. I'm afraid of it."

The priest's somber look turned to a smile, and he nodded gingerly.

"Come with me," he said after lighting the ritual candles, and Publius was led through a back room into a makeshift office.

There, various symbols of the gods hung... the ring of Amara, the scepter of Alabaster, and yes, Hieronus mighty hammer, in this circumstance forged of gold.

The priest sat down at his desk and Publius took a seat before him.

"I understand you witnessed the Day of the Knives," the priest said, "and that you are a green recruit.

"To see death in battle is one thing, but to see death in a place where it seems it does not belong is another."

"It's... not that," Publius said.

"Father... ehrm, brother... I had a question. I'm ashamed to ask..."

"There is no shame here," the priest said.

"What," Publius answered, "do you know of the undead?"

The priest grew a little rigid, sitting up in his chair. "Undead," he said. "Undead, you ask. Why, brother, do you ask such a question?"

Publius did not tell him his "friend" was Julia, the emperor's daughter, and he went to great lengths to conceal her identity. But he did tell the priest what happened, how she had vanished one afternoon and then returned in a crazed state.

But the priest only stared at him blankly. "Undead," the priest said, "if you believe in such a thing, have no real soul left. They are creatures of violence and hate. They are things and not people.

"If what you say is true, your friend is gone."

At the words, Publius stood up, inexplicably insulted.

"I will heal her," he said. "I will find a way."

And so Publius went to the library. The books were not numerous, and the parchment scrolls were of medicine and war.

Few even believed in the undead, and ghosts were considered superstition.

So what had happened to Julia? What had occurred?

Publius would find out… and he would heal her.

For as long as he was in Imperial City, he would try.

# Chapter Twenty-One

*Varius Tycho, Legionary*

The Second and the Third Peregothian, the Sixth Anthanian, and still Eioli stood.

She had driven away a legion, yes she had, and as Varius looked up at her dark walls in the light of the afternoon, he asked the gods what had occurred, and why it had been done.

How could veteran legionaries break like cowards?

It was a question that had been asked many times before, one Varius—in his short time on the campaign—had wondered but never gotten the answer to.

Aulus was gone; he had left with his legion, and now Tycho was with his, the Sixth Anthanian.

It had been his legion ever since he first donned the armor of the Empire and bore his sword. It had been posted in various places, in deserts, in green plains, in far-off northern climes where the snow and wind was biting. But here… so close to home, it had never been posted at a place so foreign, so strange. The Ugars were foreigners among foreigners. They worshipped strange gods and obeyed odd customs.

And now Varius was standing here in the hot autumn sun, sword at his side, shield strapped to his back. He was awaiting orders from a commander he did not respect, the once-councilor and now grand legate Agatho Lornodoris.

Encamped they were, but the people of Eioli were richly supplied, even fat, and they would not be breaking any time soon.

Moreover, their sister cities had joined them; there were reports far-off of scattered armies.

So it was Tycho's task to wait. It was Tycho's task to obey whatever orders had be given him.

"Hail! Varius!"

No one ever called him by his first name.

So when he turned to the voice, it was as he expected; a guard draped in a red half-cape, leaning on a spear.

He was one of Lornodoris's men.

"Please," he said, "come with me."

~

The guard took him, to his surprise, not to the tent where the grand legate was staying, but away, out into the cool of the outlying hills.

There, there were others.

One of them did not have the look of a soldier, but instead was wearing a plain black cloak.

His eyes were dark, his hair a dark brown. Around his neck was a necklace with an eagle pendant.

"Varius," he said, "I must speak with you privately.

"I understand you met with Agatho Lornodoris. We have reasons to suspect he is disobeying orders. I believe you may be able to help."

# Chapter Twenty-Two

*Varius Tycho, Legionary*

The afternoon sun shone on Tycho, and cast light upon the cypresses.

Beyond him, beyond the government agent and the guards lay the farm fields which now were untended, which the Imperials had robbed for all their worth.

"You don't trust him," Tycho repeated the agent's strange words.

The Imperial government was a behemoth, and beneath each councilor were hundreds of servants and staff, public slaves and pages. Tycho did not know this man; he did not know his face, but he assumed he had come from Imperial City.

He had no reason to question him. But he could not help his suspicion.

He was steely-eyed, confident, this man, and whatever his intentions were, Tycho did not know. The smile on his face was faint, but it was almost a smirk.

The agent reached out his hand. "I am Sextus."

Sextus had on a fine robe; he was surrounded by Imperial guards. Why would Tycho question his legitimacy?

"A pleasure," Tycho said and nodded.

"We saw him trying to dispose of this," Sextus said, and pulled from the folds of his robe a scroll. "The report you wrote on Eioli's gold.

"We stole it from him quietly. He thinks it is gone. He thinks the Council will not know what you found, Tycho."

After all this, Tycho was right in his opinions of Lornodoris. A coward, he was, a man of much luxury but little courage. He was everything wrong with the August class, a caricature of what the common thought of them.

And now anger was building in Tycho.

"Not disobedient, then," Tycho said. "Traitorous. He is a traitor!"

At his words, Sextus smile became apparent. "Yes, a traitor," he said, "and we have been watching him a while. So we have a task for you, Tycho, which only you must know about.

"Tell no one of this, not your fellow legionaries, not your closest friends."

And the suspicion returned, darkening all.

"I have posted you as his personal escort. I have elevated you—temporarily—to the status of his bodyguard. I have for you clothing and armor.

"You will hear from me regularly. I want to know everything about Lornodoris. I want you to be his shadow. Do this on behalf of the nation."

The nation. Honor. Duty.

Suspicion vanished; anger returned at the coward who was supposed to be leading the legions.

Anger was building in him at Lornodoris. Anger was building in him at the Augusts.

Lornodoris would rue his cowardice. Tycho would see to it.

# Chapter Twenty-Three

*Vello Lychicus, Councilor*

The body lay in the Council Crypt.

Constantius Pello's wife was sobbing in the corner. His adult children and their children were there with her, a gaggle of toddlers.

And Lychicus knew their pain, made worse by Constantius' disfigurement, made worse by the mystery surrounding his death.

But something was hanging over Lychicus, and the weight of the nation was upon him, for in the coming days they would have to name an emperor; in the coming days they would have to make a decision no one could agree on, or else the government would be paralyzed and the nation teeter on the brink.

He thought of that as the priest of Hieronus gave the eulogy.

"Constantius Pello," the priest droned on, "Imperial. August. But most importantly, fellow countryman. He served his years in the Council's majestic halls nobly, never with ill intent, with courage, with bravery, with honesty. In his youth, he reached the rank of tribune in our armies. And now his memory is with us even as he has passed on from this world…"

Trite words were not needed. Lychicus wanted to honor his friend, but at every moment he was pondering the disaster before them, the crisis that could not be easily quelled. The Council had not produced a candidate for the White Throne because they were bitterly divided; would a moment like this bring them together somehow?

"Constantius Pello," the priest said. "Friend. Countrymen. But most importantly, Imperial. May your eyes, closed on this earth, awaken to the glory of the heavenly realms."

From a saucer the priest drew a helping of oil; he flicked it on the corpse and at the sight his wife gave a wail, falling into weeping.

Tonight the body would be buried; tonight he would be laid to rest.

And what had occurred? They still did not know, for the physician hadn't seen anything like it; he said it looked like he had aged in the span of seconds, and that his body had shriveled and withered.

Gods help Constantius' wife and children. Gods help them all.

~

The meeting was informal; in the Council chamber, no session could be legally convened until the emperor had been nominated.

But the various factions were meeting in the light of noon, and the sun was shining down from the Oculus.

Marius Kelvus was there, and so was Faustus Chorus. Together with Lychicus, they represented the opposing groups, the opposing point of view. If they could agree on a candidate to present, an emperor would be named, and this crisis they had found themselves in would be over.

"I have proposed over and over," Lychicus began, "that we nominate Onanus, the Magister of Food and Wine."

Kelvus shook his head and grumbled some unintelligible curse.

"The Magister of Food and Wine is the least equipped of the palace cretins," Kelvus said. "I will never vote for him. All he knows is legers and weights and scales…"

But Lychicus knew he was more than that; he was wise, he was shrewd, but also he was impressionable, not one to push the bounds of the law, and the Council could keep easy control over him.

But Kelvus was not the only one fuming; a bitter look had come over Faustus Chorus.

He, representing Imperial City's affluent northern perimeter, was not one to support Onanus—a Knight and not an August, a member of the lower of the two tiers of nobility. How often he had heard Faustus Chorus speak ill of their peers—men who, though not of the highest rank, were descendants of conquerors.

"Onanus will never be emperor," said Faustus Chorus. "I will do everything in my power to oppose him."

It dawned on Lychicus that this Council of fools would never put the country ahead of their own opinions; they would concede, yes, but only on their own terms. It was an embarrassment and the Imperial nation deserved better. It deserved better, yes. It deserved councilors like Caro, like Trimalchius, like Caius Lornodoris the first of his name. But Lychicus knew this council would not serve the nation like other councils had. They were ever ambitious, ever conniving, but worst of all was their arrogance, their inability to give in even a little bit. They were strong willed and did not put the nation above their principles.

Lychicus would have to live by it. He would have to learn to concede himself, to do his best to acquiesce to whatever Faustus Chorus and Kelvus wanted.

"I propose Secundus," Kelvus answered.

The famed legate would also never secure a majority, and thinking of that soldier's haughtiness, his arrogance, his disdain for the Council and its laws, Lychicus wondered if he could swallow such a bitter pill himself.

"Never!" Lychicus said. "You heard how he addressed the Council during the Lateran War."

He could not help himself; he would never vote for a man

of such bravado, so ill tempered, so undeservedly haughty. At the thought of him anger was rising up in Lychicus, anger he could not help, anger that burst like a well from within.

"Nor will I vote for him," Faustus Chorus said, "not ever."

Kelvus was glaring at them, and then, it was at that point, that Lychicus realized they were at a grave impasse, that the nation—as it stood right now—would be paralyzed into the immediate future.

Yes, the nation deserved better. It deserved much better. Lychicus needed to find a way out of it.

~

In the Conciliar Library, the largest library outside the Eastern Kingdoms, Lychicus busied himself throughout the day poring through the Council's ancient laws and regulations.

As he read through the tomes, searching for a way out of this, it struck Lychicus that the Legis—in his career—had made several incorrect rulings, rulings that would surely be overturned if these books had been opened.

It was almost night, and the rosy light of dusk was peeking through the windows, when Lychicus found what he had been looking for.

During the Council of Attius, dated to the thirtieth year of the Empire, such an impasse was found, and the council could not name a proper candidate for the White Throne.

At that time they consulted the augurs, who—by prayer and ritual—determined who would rule.

It was law; it was precedent. Lychicus knew the councilors would have no choice but to agree.

The augurs, sorcerers of wind and speed, were also devout and steeped in religious ritual. Where thirty bickering men could not agree, the augurs would make their choice.

# Chapter Twenty-Four

*Publius Allius Corvus, Legionary*

The one day he was meant to be detained had stretched to two, then three, and now a week had gone by.

Still now he was behind the stone walls of Fort Mettius, with the tribune eagerly plying him with questions.

More memories of the Day of the Knives had returned, and as he sat at his bedside table, staring out the window, he remembered something else.

It would be of no use to the tribune, but he remembered red garbed people, flitting in and of the crowd, and of a pale-faced maiden with jet black hair.

*"Publius!"* a voice echoed and in the span of a second his chair had collapsed; he was lying on the floor, gasping.

Visions floated through his head, of a red smiling face, of a statue of black that stretched to the heavens.

The visions grew more vibrant, and then burst into a lucid dream.

~

He was in the blackness of a tunnel, and he could hear the waters dripping from up above. Below him there was stinking water, but up ahead there was a door, painted with a red hand.

And Publius himself was crawling sideways along the tunnel like a spider, breathing heavily.

And he spoke, and it was not his voice that he heard, but Julia's—raspier and hoarser but Julia's: "Maria Domina… Vitellia Procula."

When he awoke there were soldiers above him, tending to him.

He was drenched in cold sweat.

And he was repeating the words, the words he had spoken in Julia's voice: "Maria Domina… Vitellia Procula…"

The tribune was now in the room. "What is wrong, Publius?" he said, and helped him to his feet.

"I feel," Publius began, "as though I've seen a ghost."

And it came to him then, that he was seeing himself through Julia's eyes… that those words, those names, held a clue somehow. He was seeing through Julia's eyes because—though she'd been transformed in the worst way—her gift remained, her ability to appear to people. Perhaps, that gift had become twisted in light of the state she was in.

~

"Just a dream," Publius said, "a bad dream."

They were in the interrogation room. Across from Publius, a candle was flickering. On the other side of the table was the prelate.

"And what was your dream?" the prelate said.

Why did he need to know? "I was crawling… through tunnels… through stinking water…"

"The sewers?" the prelate said. "I believe this situation is having an ill effect on you. I think you've done all you can to help our investigation. We are sending you to Eioli in the morning."

"But Julia—" Publius said without thinking.

But the prelate answered with a mocking smile. "Julia? A 'good friend?' She will be here when you get back."

*Those teasing words…*

"No," Publius said. "That's not it at all."

But how could he stay? How could he convince them?

"I have things to do," Publius said.

The prelate seemed indignant at the words. "Things to do. Yes. You took an oath, remember? Your country demands you in Eioli."

Yes, his oath, he forgot, one he had taken before he departed for Blue Eagle camp all that time ago. An oath to the nation, to the people of the Empire, to its laws—writ in tablets of stone.

But an oath he had taken also to the emperor. Marcus Seánus was dead but the White Throne was vacant. He would help Julia. He would rescue her.

He had no other choice.

# Chapter Twenty-Five

*Publius Allius Corvus, Legionary*

Publius slipped away in the dead of the night.

He was wearing his plainclothes, and though his hair was trim in the manner of the soldier, he intended to keep away at all times from public view.

The stone avenues and thoroughfares of Imperial City were lit by streetlamps, and he knew the urban cohorts did regular patrols, but the city was largely unprotected at night, a wild jungle of crime and underhanded transactions.

But it was here, in the darkness of the night, that Julia was like to approach him.

"Julia," Publius said, "why do I care so much about you?"

He had his sword buckled to his side but all other ornament of the legionary was gone. He was in plainclothes, and the holy symbol that had belonged to his father he clutched in his hand.

If she came to him, he would confront her; he would try to drive out whatever was inside her, to purge her of the state she was in.

The priest denied he could help her. The books in the library said nothing of the topic.

But when he had confronted her the first time, when he had well and truly confronted her, he had seen some of the darkness that drove her dissipate. He had seen her pallid white hair turn a shade of blonde; he had seen the underworldly gleam in her eyes wane.

"Where are you?" Publius said, lingering in the shadows between streetlamps.

But there was no sign of her.

He pulled his cloak a bit tighter around him. The night was

cold, and there was a hint of winter to its chill.

"Julia," he said, "Julia… come to me."

But there was no response, only the ambient noises of the night, the distant murmur of sounds, carriages rattling and dull music emanating from Imperial Square.

~

Imperial Square was a different place in the night than it was in the day.

Up above the buildings, advertisements for elixirs and medicines were painted.

Before the Imperial Treasury and the Hall of Justice were innumerable street lamps of painted glass, red, green, blue.

And the square was filled with people, yes it was. But it was a different crowd than the people of the day; the people of the night were here.

Music was spilling out from all corners, lyres, lutes, drums. Prostitutes in furs were just ahead. On the street, two men were playing dice and betting piles of coins.

Above the noise of chatting voices, the notes of a lute and lyre rose up, singing voices underneath the stars.

And though it was a place of iniquity, a place filled with illicit entertainments and underhanded transactions done in the dark, it was a place of nocturnal, almost supernal beauty.

The activity would continue at all hours, even into the morning. In Imperial City, there was no curfew like there was in the country. Imperial City was a place that never halted, not day or night.

And Publius was here, in the square, at night, for the first time he could remember.

In the distance, a pair of ratlings were shifting through the crowd.

There were people there who looked too young, a boy and a girl kissing beneath a statue. And amid the gaggle was a man whose hair was cut in a tonsure—was it a monk who had slipped away from the monastery for a bit of immoral fun?

Surrounding Imperial Square were public buildings, great monuments to the Imperial government. There was the hippodrome, great and vast but now dark and silent. They were like shadows in the night, unlit and black, with their contours visible as silhouettes.

It was a good place for Publius to remain. Tomorrow, the urban cohorts would surely issue a warrant for his arrest.

He had made his choice; he had done this for Julia.

And as he walked through the crowd past the revelers, past the prostitutes in their tunics offering services, past the gambling tables and the young people guzzling wine, he noted something out of the corner of his eye, something he hadn't seen before.

Standing there, in the crowd, were two people garbed in red, a man and a woman, speaking to a child who looked impressionable.

The shape of their cloaks and the color reminded him of the Day of the Knives.

Those assassins would surely not recognize Publius; they would not know who he was.

He drew near them, stopping just inches away. Amid the dull rancor of the crowd, he could just barely hear their conversation.

"The Red Lord loves children," the woman was saying. "Children are often wiser than their parents. They know more than them. They are more understanding.

"Your parents are leading you astray… the Red Dawn is coming. It is coming soon. And when the Red Dawn comes you will be rescued and your parents will be caught in the storm."

He turned to see the child looking up at them.

How could a child so young be in Imperial Square at night? It was dangerous even for someone of Publius' age.

"My parents will be in the storm?" the child said, clearly not understanding.

These cultists were feeding him things, things that weren't true.

But the color of their dress—a crimson red—was identical to what he'd seen in the Day of the Knives, and so he felt himself immobilized, unable or unwilling to help.

"Where are the keys to your house?" the woman said. "Did you bring them to us like a good boy?"

At the words, Publius drew his sword and charged forward. "Go away!" Publius said to the child. "Run! These are bad people!"

And the child, holding the keys in his hands, did just that, scurrying away into the dark.

The red-garbed woman was now wielding a curved dagger.

"Try me," Publius said. "Try to face me… a soldier of the Empire. I'm not a bystander on an autumn afternoon. I'm not an unsuspecting victim to plunge that knife into."

The woman began to back away. "The Red Dawn is coming, fool," she said, but her voice was quaking and she was clearly shaken. "The Red Dawn is coming."

"The Red Dawn, whatever you call it, is never coming," Publius said, "and one day the long arm of justice will find you. One day it will… mark my words, scum."

He lurched forward, as if to strike, and the cultists went sprinting through the crowd. Publius laughed at them as they disappeared into the darkness.

But he had not lost sight of his mission of why he had come.

Criminals, they were indeed, and terrible people who would deceive a child…. But Publius was at odds with the law.

For Julia's sake he had broken the law. For his oath he had

broken the law, on behalf of it—for part was to protect the emperor and his family, the emperor, who embodied the nation. The emperor was its face, its representative.

Publius was walking past the revelers, past the prostitutes and their solicitations. Julia surely would have found him by now. She had found him so easily; wasn't she still looking for him?

On the edge of the Imperial Square, where it was met by a dark street, a woman had set up shop.

A foldable table was there, and on it a black glass. On her head was some sort of purple-colored headwrap. She was swarthy, a southron no doubt.

Across from her was a woman, much younger, fairer of skin, an Imperial. Her hands were outstretched, and the southron woman was touching them.

"Friend," the southron said. "Let us ask the spirits. Who will Laria marry? Tell us, O spirits…"

And Publius felt a twinge of bad air, a sickening feeling, and an urge to run.

"No husband shall Laria have." The southron's voice was deep, now. "No husband at all. She shall grow horns on her head. She shall rise up, and black like coals shall be her eyes…"

Publius walked away, thinking on the words but glad to be away. What was the name of the Ugars' god? Belpheor?

Then Publius remembered the dream he'd had, crawling in subterranean tunnels. The sewer, the depository of Imperial City's waste and effluent—could that be where Julia was?

Staggered by whatever force he felt, he thought twice about hiding in this crowd, though there was no better place to hide.

By chance he looked up, and there in the moonlight, on

the face of a great brick building, he saw an advertisement painted: "Elixirs and Healing by Vitellia Procula."

An image accompanied the text, of a woman raven hair, holding a glass vial. Below the text was an address on Fullers Street in the Villa Fort ward.

Vitellia Procula… he had heard himself, or Julia, say those very words.

"Maria Domina… Vitellia Procula." Those were the words he'd heard Julia say in his dream.

Perhaps, they were a warning from her, or a clue.

Tomorrow, in the light of day, he would go there. Tomorrow, he would find out just who Vitellia Procula was.

# Chapter Twenty-Six

*Varius Tycho, Imperial Guard*

Being sworn into the Imperial Guard, even if only temporarily, was surely a change.

And as he stood there with a spear in one hand and a shield in the other, watching over Agatho Lornodoris in his tent, he realized it was a change he did not like, a change he did not welcome.

For over the days that he had guarded Lornodoris, he had found himself in a different world: a world not of the camps, of the hardy lives of soldiers, but of luxury, ambition, and daggers in the dark.

Lornodoris was writing on parchment. It seemed to be all he did.

Writs and letters required his signature, and even far afield from the Imperial Council, he seemed to busy himself with the work of the nation.

And as Tycho watched silently, he realized he had come to despise this man, this oaf.

For Tycho was no August, nor was he a Knight. There was no nobility in his line. He had been born in the Harbor District of Imperial City; he had grown up in a shanty home. And he was proud of his common origins. Everything he had he had earned. Everything he achieved was due to his own hand, and those of the gods.

Lornodoris looked up from his writing.

"Varius Tycho," he said.

The formality made Tycho even more angry.

A candle was lighting his work. Night had fallen and the camp was silent.

"Yes, Signor Legate?" Tycho said. It was more respect than he deserved.

"In the coming days, you will accompany me on a secret mission," Lornodoris said. "I have orders from the Imperial Council. We will make peace with the King of Eioli.

"The Ugars have signaled their interest in ending this war."

At the news Tycho could feel his hackles raise, his anger bursting forth. The Imperial Council, those thirty fools, had no idea of honor, of what such a concession would to do the soldiers' pride. But they never cared about soldiers, about legionaries; they viewed them as pawns in their hands and nothing more.

"Ending the war," Tycho said. "A wise choice."

At all times, he kept an air of respect that he did not feel, for the more Lornodoris would trust him, the more he would tell him.

~

The morning light was shining in on the tent; its dull glow gave a more cheerful look to Tycho's spare quarters. He rose from his cot and heard in the distance a horn—three percussive notes. It was his sign.

Lornodoris was no doubt still asleep. In addition to being a coward, he was also a sluggard, and while the common legionaries were up before dark, he seemed not to be able to rise until well after the sun began to shine.

And so, Tycho quickly dressed himself, laying over his breastplate and his red half cape, grabbing his spear and sword, and his buckler.

He left in the garb of an Imperial Guard, and he ventured outside the tent into the cool air.

Sextus was waiting for him in the hills.

He was dressed as he was before in the dark brown cloak. It was partially open, and he was wearing a tunic of jet-black wool beneath it, a tunic embroidered with a stylized eye.

"What do you have to report?" he said.

They had not met in several days.

"Lornodoris intends to sue for peace," Tycho said. "He is as honorless as I thought. But I did not expect the Imperial Council to give in to the Ugars."

Sextus appeared shocked, and then anger appeared in his dark eyes. "The Imperial Council made no such directive. He is deceiving you.

"Tell me, Tycho, what would you do for the Empire?"

"There is no limit to my service," Tycho said, "and there is no day my oath expires."

From the folds of his dull cloak, Sextus pulled a knife with a thin blade, so small it could fit in his pocket.

"Take this," Sextus said, "and wait for further orders."

Tycho knew what his action was implying.

But what he spoke was true; there was no limit to his service, and no day his oath expired.

# Chapter Twenty-Seven

*Publius Allius Corvus, Legionary*

The day's light brought new fears and worries. He had slept in Imperial Square beside a pile of crates.

And now, walking amid the rosy dawn as vendors set up their stalls and merchants began to move in, he remembered what he had done and the sacrifice he had made.

And for now, it had been for naught. Julia had not approached him, no, she hadn't. He hoped to the gods nothing had happened to her. He hoped she had not attacked the wrong person, someone stronger than Publius and more violent.

Then he remembered the name Vitellia Procula, and of the advertisement he had seen painted on a brick walls.

He had heard Julia utter that name in his dream, with the equally strange name "Maria Domina."

He recalled it was an advertisement for an elixir shop, and he remembered its location in the ward of Villa Fort.

And, scanning for signs of the urban cohort, he quickly departed.

In the light of day, in the light of his changed status of a fugitive, Imperial City was different, and though life had largely returned after the Day of the Knives, it was a different sort of life—people seemed more subdued and untrusting, not meeting eye contact with Publius as he walked by. At all corners there was an air of fear and people seemed on edge, hurrying from place to place with their heads down, eager to get home—fearing there was a red-garbed assassin behind every member of the crowd, waiting to strike with a knife.

And as he passed by, he also sensed anger hanging just beneath the fear—anger that the Imperial Council had not arrested the perpetrators, anger that the urban cohorts had not doubled their patrols… a fact Publius was thankful for.

Villa Fort was on the far edge of the city; it was a forgotten ward, free from the sea-breezes and gusts, a cluster of apartments and shops built among hills. Publius had been there before in his youth, but had not often gone. He wondered if it had changed.

~

The homes of Villa Fort were a mixture of rich and poor, but even the apartment blocks that housed the masses had bright red-roof tiles, and its concrete was a shade of brown. The sun was shining; it was an autumn day, but a light wind was blowing from the north, and it was chilly in character.

But as he navigated his way down the road, inquiring of people in the crowd, he learned the location of the apothecary that Vitellia Procula ran.

He already had it planned out. He would go into the shop, linger a long while, pretend to be searching for something for a cold. He would talk as much as he could. He would try to learn as much as he would.

He would learn, he hoped, if Julia had been trying to tell him something.

The shop was massive, taking up an entire city block.

A horsedrawn carriage was sitting before the great door. Rich people were ambling by—rich people, garbed in silken tunics and thick breeches, women in great billowing gowns.

Procula's customers, and probably the owner herself, were rich.

And Publius had been the rich boy on Seafarers' Way, but that said little. Here there were great villas blocked by iron-grilled fences, and there was a green park in the distance.

But Publius had a task to finish, a task to find Julia, to bring her back from whatever dark state she had been plunged into.

Publius walked through the doors of Procula's shop, and found within a hall of marble, a desk, and behind it a vault filled with shelves. On the shelves were glass vials and jars, gleaming in the light of the candles. And behind the desk was a young woman dressed in a plain brown gown.

This was not Procula, for her hair was blond and not black. She was not who Publius sought.

"May I help you, signore?" the woman said, and for a moment, Publius paused.

He hadn't thought it all through. A cold was not enough to distract. What could occupy her time?

And far in the corner, at that very moment—he saw it, behind the shelves, a red-painted hand.

It was the same style he'd seen painted on the tavern wall.

Who was this Procula? Did she have something to do with the assassins? Was she involved in the Day of the Knives?

"My friend," Publius blurted out. "She is… she is gone."

He tried to come up with a sickness, some terrible disease that was believable. Malaria, perhaps, or black fever.

"Gone?" The attendant's voice was now a whisper. "So you have heard. Who told you?

"It does not matter. But know that such services are very expensive. You will need a private meeting with Domina Procula."

What did she mean? It did not matter. A meeting with Domina Procula was what he had sought.

He hoped against hope that Julia had led him here. He hoped against hope the name "Vitellia Procula" meant something.

Julia had not let him down before.

But the attendant was staring at him, waiting for a response, and Publius—blindsided—had not given her what she had asked for.

"Yes, yes," Publius said. "I am young but I am a rich man. I will be able to pay whatever price Domina Procula requires."

What was this service she was offering?

"It is urgent," Publius said. "I will pay double whatever you require…"

The woman pursed her lips, as if she were pondering in her own mind.

She retreated into the shadows. Publius heard a door open and close.

~

He was waiting for what seemed an hour.

But eventually, the woman returned.

She had a mousy look on her face.

"You are a soldier," she said. "Your haircut…"

"Yes, I am in the legion," Publius said. "A centurion, in fact."

How else could he explain the money he supposedly had? Centurions were rich, weren't they?

"We do not serve soldiers," she said. "Goodbye."

When she said "goodbye," there was a caustic edge to her voice.

They did not serve soldiers? Publius had never heard of such a policy.

But he would respect her wishes. What could he do besides respect her wishes?

As he lingered among the streets of Villa Fort in the waning heat of the day, he thought to himself, and he wondered, just what this special "service" was.

And he wondered if he had merely hid his short-trimmed

hair, styled in the manner of a legionary, if he could have deceived the attendant and met with Vitellia Procula.

He found himself at dusk walking into the doors of a tavern. What better way was there to forget his defeat?

# Chapter Twenty-Eight

*Publius Allius Corvus, Legionary*

The tavern was called the "House of the Laurel."

Compared to the squalid establishments of Mud Bottom, it was a veritable palace; its floors were of marble, and there were many tables and booths of teak, all filled to the capacity. Before the bar was a fountain bubbling with water. Behind the bar was a rack filled with hundreds of wine bottles.

The "House of the Laurel" was bustling with activity, even this early, even at dusk; and though every table was full of people, Publius spotted—out of the corner of his eye—a seat at the bar that had not been claimed.

The soldier's life had not been what he'd always wanted, but now, Publius did not lack money, and as he hurried to the seat he could feel the coins of copper and silver jingling in his coinpurse.

What better place was there to spend an eve of failure, overshadowed with worry, than at a tavern, the "House of the Laurel" nonetheless.

The barkeep was a pudgy man with greasy brown hair. His eyes were blue, and as he approached, Publius noted his apron was stained with grease. Perhaps, he also fancied himself a cook, or—at a minimum—a kitchen manager.

"What will you have?" he said.

"Korthian red," Publius said.

At such a desperate moment, why not the best in stock?

"Very well," the barkeep said. "A soldier, are you? A legionary?"

"The Sixth Anthanian," Publius said. "I'm on leave."

And in a way, it was not a lie; he was on leave, but a leave of his own choosing.

"On leave," the barkeep repeated. His eyes were droll, and they lingered on him. He turned, grabbing a glass and wiping it with a cloth.

Publius watched as the barkeep uncorked a great bottle; he watched as the lush red liquid poured from it and began to slowly fill up the glass. His mouth watered at the sight.

He felt a hand brush his shoulder.

He turned to see a man standing there, young and lithe, no older than twenty. His eyes were dark and his frame was slight and slender.

"A word…" His voice was weak and soft. "A word, please… It is urgent."

With a glass of Korthian red finally in hand, Publius reluctantly acquiesced.

The young man led him through the great hall, past tables and chairs and booths, and into a dark hidden room that was ill lit and sparely decorated.

"I saw you at the elixery," the man said. "At Maria Domina's shop."

"Maria Domina?" Publius said. "It said her name was Vitellia Procula."

"That is her legal name," the man said. "But everyone who knows her knows what she likes to be called… Maria Domina. She is a rich woman, but she is a thief, and a liar, and a criminal. She is a sorceress, too, and the worst kind… a necromancer, a dealer in death."

Publius felt his eyes widen. He was trying to make sense of it but he supposed he couldn't. A sorceress… a necromancer. And why was this man telling him all this? Why was he so concerned for Publius, whom he did not know?

"Who are you?" Publius said.

"I am Caeso," the young man said. "That is what you can call me. I am one of her victims. I believed her lies…

"Now I keep watch on others. I warn them of her."

Lies. Sorcery. Necromancy.

Such a tale seemed woven from the mind of a great storyteller. But he believed Caeso.

Necromancy was the stuff of legends, and not something many believed in. Many had witnessed the powers of the augurs, and some the flamens, but few if any had witnessed those sorcerers with power over death.

"She is a leader in the Cult of the Red Hand," Caeso continued. "She is in charge of all the members in Imperial City. She hates the Empire. Everyone in the Red Hand does; they believe they must destroy it to usher in the new world order."

"The Red Hand?" Publius said. He recalled the insignia. He had been right. "And the Day of the Knives…"

"She organized the massacre," Caeso said. "I am sure of it. Her fingers are all over it."

Publius now had a witness. He did not want to drag Caeso before the prelate, but he might have to. He seemed to have some connection to the Red Hand cult.

"The Red Dawn," Caeso said. "That is what they believe in. They believe they must first kill the emperor, he who sits on the Red Throne. Then the Red Lord will appear—"

The Red Lord. The Red Lord! Julia had said those words.

"—and soon after he appears, the world will burn away. All will be remade. And a new order will be ushered in…"

Julia's request to him had been to go to Saturnus Rock, to proclaim "The Red Lord cometh."

Surely, Julia of all people, Julia Seánus, the emperor's daughter, a member of the most blueblooded of blueblooded families, would not so disgrace herself. She could not be involved in the Red Hand cult, a cult which—by their very words—sought to kill the emperor.

"Julia—" He spoke her name, and Caeso's eyes lit up.

"Yes, Julia Seánus… she was one of us. She—" He became quiet, lips sealed shut. Suddenly, suspicion seemed to come over him, a lack of trust. "I've said too much."

He got up from his seat. "I came to warn you. Get out of here. Maria Domina hates soldiers; she believes they are the agents of the Empire. You have a target on your back, now, my good man.

"Tell no one of me. Tell no one I told you. I was in the Red Hand cult; I believed in the Red Dawn. But I escaped… and now I fear if she catches me she will turn me into a Strig…"

"What is a Strig?" Publius began to say, but Caeso was already leaving the room.

Publius finished the remainder of his Korthian wine in the dark. He then left the raucous laughter and noise of the "House of the Laurel." He would sleep outside. He was not afraid of Maria Domina. He would not have her out of his sights.

~

The night was cool, and clouds covered the sky for the first time in a long while. A wintry breeze was blowing and a light misting rain began.

Publius had chosen a sleeping place in the middle of an alley.

And as he sat there, the words of Caeso were hovering over him.

A "Strig"… what was that? Publius felt he had heard of the word before. But where had he heard it?

After serious thought, he recalled a story from a babysitter, an older child from Seafarers' Way who had watched over him when Father and Mother were gone.

The Strig haunted a village. The hero he could not remember. But just what was the Strig? What kind of creature was it? He remembered the Strig from the story, how it had ambushed people on the road and stolen away their life, and for each year it took it grew a little stronger and a little bolder.

"The Strig of Formia"… that was what the story was called.

He remembered how much it had scared him as a child.

A shadow was perched in between the alleyway up ahead.

In the dark light of the streetlamps it was a silhouette, but Publius recognized its gait, the twisted way it stood up on its legs.

It was the thing that had been hunting him… the dark spirit or wraith which had taken control of Julia.

But would he help Julia now, knowing she had been a part of the Red Cult, knowing she had betrayed her father?

Perhaps, it was best to put an end to her altogether.

Yet Publius did not draw his sword.

From his neck, he removed his father's holy symbol, the holy hammer of Hieronus.

And as he approached boldly, briskly, without a hint of fear, he could sense the fear in the creature, in the being that was in control of Julia's body.

Yet its response to fear was to charge him, to sprint at him with its awkward legs.

In the light he saw her face, or what little he could see of it, the eyes black like marbles, the white colorless hair, the skin as pale as snow. The stench of death was overwhelming when she was met head on with the holy symbol.

She grimaced at the sight of it, but she could not push past it.

He raised the holy symbol; he pushed onwards, ahead. Color returned to strands of her hair; whites grew in her eyes. And she fell over, onto her side, weeping. It was her voice, again now, the voice he recognized: "Oh, Publius, what have I done?"

Like that he knew, and in an instant he was convinced, that whatever he was looking at was a Strig, and that Maria Domina had done this to her. So how could he avenge her? How could he make this right?

As he saw her weeping, returned just momentarily to her innocent state, he vowed anew to rescue her, that whatever she had done and whatever she had intended before this, he would help her. He would decimate the Red Hand cult. And if Julia could not be helped, then, why, he would see his sword plunged through Maria Domina's heart. A more wicked woman, a more contemptible sorceress, the Empire had never produced.

"I will help you," Publius said. It was a vow; an oath he intended to keep.

It was an oath he held as sacred as his soldier's oath.

"I will help you," Publius said once more, but Julia—or the Strig—was now long gone.

"I will help you!"

# Chapter Twenty-Nine

*Vello Lychicus, Councilor*

The Council was not legally convened; its pronouncements had no weight. Until they identified a candidate for the White Throne, there would be no votes.

But twenty-nine were gathered in the Council House, underneath the light of the Oculus; twenty-nine were present , including Lychicus, and all—in their own way, in their own incorrigible way—were trying to navigate their way out of this crisis. As he stood before them, he tried to remember there was no malice or ill will.

Lychicus was sitting; in the center of the room Councilor Saius was standing. He too was trying to earnestly wrest his way out of this impasse.

But Lychicus had not spoken. No, he had not spoken; and he was ready.

"We cannot agree," Saius said, "not even at this moment, not even at this time of peril. When wars rage in Ugarit, when barbarians threaten the north… not even now can we put our pride aside."

"It does not matter," Lychicus said boldly, "what we think or do. For precedent is already set. I ask for the floor."

Saius nodded. There was no reason for rules or regulations; it was a habit, but the Legis was not present. The government was paralyzed, but still they could not help themselves. They were acting as if this were a legal session, as if procedure had to be followed.

~

But when Lychicus opened the book, and told them of the

precedent, that such an incident had occurred before, no one raised objection. Tradition was still to be followed; tradition was still honored in these majestic halls.

They agreed to nominate whoever the augurs appointed, and with that mandate Lychicus left.

He would go to the cave outside the city bounds where the augurs met. He would ask the Wind Lord for his consent.

And the Wind Lord's word would be law.

# Chapter Thirty

*Publius Allius Corvus, Legionary*

The morning light shone down on Imperial City, and Publius awoke in the alley safe—in the knowledge that he was a fugitive, but safe.

So where should he go, and who should he turn to, now that he knew that Julia—wherever she was—was a Strig?

He thought of his brothers and sisters. He wondered if Marcus had boarded the next ship to Haroon. He wondered if Julia would hunt them down, the family Corvus, just because they were related.

But that was not what was pressing on his mind.

He looked out into the light beyond the alleyway, and amid the crowd saw a man of the urban cohorts, wearing a leather jerkin and a soldier's helmet. The sun glinted on the glossy metal, and the horsehair crest was a vibrant red, the color of blood.

Publius would be considered a deserter, at least until he explained the situation, and even then he'd surely be punished—demoted, fined, or something.

But the man of the urban cohorts quickly vanished into the crowd.

~

It was a bright morning and the people of Villa Fort were going about their business.

The sun was out but there was a chill in the air.

Publius had his sword buckled to his side.

He thought again of Julia, and then remembered what he had seen, what he had witnessed… Vitellia Procula, the leader of the Cult of the Red Hand.

Caeso, the young man who'd escaped the cult's grip.

And talk of something that had no explanation… what these deranged people called the "Red Dawn."

Some still spoke of the day the skies in Imperial City turned red. Could that be what these fools were talking about?

"Pardon, signore!" shouted a voice. Publius turned and his heart twisted as he saw it was a man of the urban cohorts, dressed in leather.

"On leave, are you?" he said and a bit of the fear melted away. He had no idea. "We saw you, signore, in the shop of Vitellia Procula. Would you mind coming to the legion post to answer questions?"

Like a snake darting into the underbrush, Publius was gone, vanishing into the crowd, hurrying through the mélange of faces and fabrics.

But as he hurried away from the soldier, it dawned on him that the eyes of the law were on Vitellia Procula, that somehow—some way—they were closing in on her.


After hurrying ahead for what seemed like an hour, Publius came up against a great stone wall, and he saw that he was now at the western edge of Villa Fort.

The bounds of Imperial City ended here, but beyond there were clustered towns and villages, a suburban sprawl that surrounded it for miles.

He was tempted to leave altogether, to leave Julia and everything behind, but he knew it wasn't possible.

"Signore."

The words jolted him out of his focus, but he quickly calmed down and managed to collect his thoughts.

A man was approaching, walking down a side street.

His tunic was jet black. Around his neck was a gold necklace shaped like an eye.

Who was this man? He had no idea.

His hair was trimmed neatly, a dark brown. His eyes were silvery and his breeches had many pockets.

"A word of advice, Publius Corvus… Look down below."

He gestured to the sewer main, a bronze covering emblazoned with the eagle insignia of the Empire.

And like that, confusion turned to fear, and as he wondered just what this strange man meant, he felt himself hurrying, half-running, half-walking away.

But those words also planted something into his mind. And he remembered his dream, the one that had terrified him… he, behind the eyes of Julia, crawling through the Imperial City sewers.

# Chapter Thirty-One

*Vello Lychicus, Councilor*

The cave where the Wind Lord resided was on a mountainous outcrop several miles outside the city bounds. To reach the summit of this high hill, which Lychicus had achieved, one had to leave his horse and do rigorous climbing.

But panting and haggard, though his muscles ached and his old bones were gnawing with pain, Lychicus had achieved it.

He, the representative of the Imperial Council, had reached his destination. At the age of seventy-five, he had climbed to the Cave of Time and Wind.

Various augurs were standing there… men and women in winged leather helmets and leather armor. They were leaning on their quarterstaffs as he approached.

But Lychicus turned and looked outwards. Beyond the pines and cypresses, across many hilltop villages and towns, one could just barely make out in the horizon the smoke of Imperial City. It was a dark color against a vast canvas. It was deceptively close; the journey had taken Lychicus the better part of a day.

He turned back to the augurs, and as they stood there he felt a light wind gusting all about, touching his skin and ruffling his hair.

The male augur was tall and broad shouldered, with blue eyes.

"Councilor Lychicus?" he said. Wind seemed to swirl about him, and his winged boots seemed to levitate whenever there was movement. In his hand was a thin staff.

"Yes," Lychicus said. "I am he."

"Come with me," the augur answered.

And so Lychicus followed him, though he was slow and the

augur was as swift as the wind. Into the Cave of Time and Wind he walked. When he returned, the White Throne would not long sit empty.

~

"We have been expecting you," the augur said.

More of his kind were in the vast cave, augurs young and old, augurs male and female. Some were sitting at tables; others were standing guard, posted at various doors.

Lychicus wondered how the news had traveled so quickly, how they already knew he was coming, and, presumably, what he was coming for.

The augur turned and again his winged boots seemed to just barely grace the ground. His blue eyes darkened a bit. "I wish it were in better circumstances that you had arrived," he said.

"I know—" Lychicus started.

But the augur cut him off: "The Wind Lord has died. Last night, he was seized by a virulent tremor. In the morning he was dead."

His expression became grim.

"We will give him the rites in the name of Anemon tonight, at dusk."

Lychicus recalled the augurs worshipped the god Anemon, lord of wind and speed, depicted as a man with an eagle's head. He was obscure and no one worshiped him outside the augur order.

The augur gripped his staff a bit tighter. "In the meantime, a replacement is appointed. He will take the reading for you."

~

A stairway led up a dank corridor through several stories. Rooms and hallways were everywhere, and alcoves with statues of

Anemon within them, lit with candles. But eventually the stairway led him into the open air, into the open sky, above the Cave of Time and Wind.

There, an augur stood. He was stocky and dark eyed, and as he gripped his quarterstaff it seemed to Lychicus that he was clumsy, and there was no wind about him. Yet this was the Wind Lord's replacement.

He hoped the reading would be good; but he knew anyone they chose would be better than the White Throne sitting empty… or, at least, he wanted to believe that.

The clumsy augur stepped forward, and Lychicus watched as he drew two stone die.

A circle was there before them, carved into the stone.

"Phillippus," the Wind Lord's replacement said. "Leave us be."

The other augur turned and nodded, and headed back into the stairwell. Lychicus was now alone, and questions began to percolate in his mind, but he kept them to himself.

"Anemon," the leader of the augurs said, "guide my hands."

He cast the die on the floor and wind gusted upwards.

The dice fell, one on the "one" mark and the other on the "three" mark.

The die read five and two.

"Anemon has spoken," the leader of the augurs continued. And like that, he made his pronouncement.

~

The name was not one Lychicus recognized, not one he had ever heard before.

But the augur wrote the name on a slip of parchment, and indicated the choice of the augur order was final.

At dusk, Lychicus left with his attendants. When he got back to Imperial City, it would be night.

# Chapter Thirty-Two

*Varius Tycho, Imperial Guard*

As the personal bodyguard of someone who deserved contempt, Tycho had learned to bite his tongue.

As he stood guard in the private tent of the oafish Agatho Lornodoris, watching him scribble furiously on his desk, he recalled his meeting with Sextus many days and nights ago, and the thin knife he still had hidden in his cloak pocket. What a good day for the Empire it would be when he finally used it.

Lornodoris was already plotting the retreat; he still had not informed the legionaries, perhaps knowing they would be indignant at the dishonor.

"Tell me, Tycho." Lornodoris was looking up at Tycho dotingly, never realizing the hatred he had for him.

"I must ask your opinion on something," he said. He looked up and his eyes seemed weak; in the days since Tycho had guarded him, he had noticed an increasing frailty.

"I must ask your opinion on the matter of war… for that, Varius Tycho, is your trade."

Tycho drew near; he could not bring himself to smile. "It is my trade," he said. "It is the trade I have known since my youth."

"And you are good at it, then, and experienced," Lornodoris said, "far more experienced than I.

"Few in the Council know war. Not many have seen it up close. But now I have, and the reality has been illuminating.

"It has been troubling to see the rigors. I do not believe you are supplied properly.

"But tell me, Tycho, the Imperial Council has accepted the Ugars' terms of peace. But I fear the men of Forward Camp would like a victory."

Tycho knew all about his lies, how he was a rogue actor, how the Imperial Council had said none of this.

When he was appointed leader of this or that battalion, he'd punish lying with flogging, or worse. Everyone knew not to lie to him. It was what he hated most.

"Tell me, Tycho, in your experience as a man of war... Should I resist? Should I, by my authority as commander of all armies, tell them 'no'? Now, it is yours to decide."

Surely, he was toying with him. Tycho was common; Lornodoris was August. He would never heed the advice of a subordinate.

And so he told him exactly what he wanted to hear. "Follow the letter of the law, Signor Legate," Tycho said. "That is what we men of war defend... the law, and peace, and order."

Lornodoris seemed almost disappointed.

From deceptive tongues often came knives. As Lornodoris looked away, Tycho felt in his pocket, seeing that the length of steel was still here.

*When, Sextus? When?*

Perhaps, hating Lornodoris was ill advised. And yet he seemed to exemplify everything that was wrong with the August class, with those who lorded over the Knights and the common. They were the descendants of the first Imperials, privileged at birth, but so often they disappointed.

"We leave today, two hours after noon," Lornodoris said. "The King of Eioli and of all Ugarit is meeting us at the palace. A treaty will be signed. They will become an ally, but not a Friend of the Empire."

What a world it was, where becoming an ally was less oppressive than becoming one's "Friend."

But Tycho, even Tycho—a common legionary—knew that "Friends of the Empire" were slaves.

A horn blew, a crisp horn.

"My Signor Legate," he said, "I must—erm—relieve myself."

"Return quickly," Lornodoris said.

# Chapter Thirty-Three

*Varius Tycho, Imperial Guard*

Sextus was waiting for him amid the gold hills.

With him were a coterie of men who resembled him, wearing dark cloaks of varying hues and knives hanging from sheaths on their belts.

And a few of the bodyguard were there, men dressed in breastplates with red half-capes over their shoulders. Not all were expected to attend to the Grand Legate at all times.

"Tycho," Sextus said, "your time is come."

Tycho nodded. But at the words, which he had now confirmed, he felt a nervousness he'd never felt before. Anxiety began to creep into his gut, a worm wriggling in his stomach.

And again suspicion returned. It was a strange mission to assassinate the sitting Speaker of the Council who—by force of law—was serving in place of the emperor.

But in Imperial City there were underhanded dealings, and it was a place of conspiracy and subterfuge. So was it not beyond possibility that the Speaker of the Council had been named a public enemy?

Who was he kidding? Of course it was true, all of it. Sextus was a man of the Imperial government. And Agatho Lornodoris was both a law-breaker and a liar.

"I am at your service," Tycho said. "At the Empire's service."

"Wait until the signing ceremony," Sextus said. "Then run, as fast as you can, to the gate. The way will be cleared by our men."

Tycho noted that on the shoulders of the men's cloaks there was a faint insignia of an eye.

"Very well," Tycho said. He could feel his hands trembling.

He had never been this anxious before, not in the Lateran War or during the Siege of Kallistis. This was all new: the state-sanctioned murder of an Imperial citizen. He still could not wrap his mind around it.

But he would do it, for the sake of his oath; he would do it for the Empire.

# Chapter Thirty-Four

*Publius Allius Corvus, Legionary*

It was high noon.

There was a clap of thunder, and as if in answer, a drizzle began to fall.

Publius had—as far as he knew—managed to escape detection. He was in Villa Fort as the rain fell down, but the crowds which had once hid him splendidly were beginning to disperse.

Abovehead, clouds had rolled in, bringing in their gloom.

Winter was coming, if it had not already come.

There was a shout.

He turned, and a man of the urban cohorts was running toward him from the distance. "You there! You! Are you Publius Corvus?"

And Publius turned and ran, sprinting through the streets, and the soldier began to run after him.

He sprinted and sprinted as fast as he could, ignoring the shouting behind him, ignoring the shocked stares of the citizens of Villa Fort. He ran and ran… and then he ran, almost, into a great stone wall.

He drew his sword, not knowing whatever else to do, turning do see the man of the urban cohorts had almost crossed the distance between them.

And then he looked down and saw a sewer main that was slightly ajar.

He recalled the words of the darkly-dressed man. He recalled the dream he'd had. And he thought it was almost meant to be.

He laid hold of the edge of the sewer main and ripped it off. A stench, nauseating and powerful, wafted up, but he cared not.

He leapt into the darkness. He landed with a splash.

~

The sewers of Imperial City connected all its parts, and with regularity water from the aqueducts would wash the filth—with great force—into the sea.

It was almost pitch black, but as his eyes adjusted Publius could see just faintly a dim illumination up ahead.

A shadow darted by and he screamed—had he just imagined it?

The stench was nauseating and he felt himself retch.

But the man of the urban cohorts shouted: "Stop! You are under arrest!" and began to make his way down into the darkness.

Publius charged ahead, splashing carelessly, not heeding the darkness or the muck.

He ran toward the illumination, whatever it was, and saw the foul waters glint at its light. He ran faster than before, half running, half wading, as fast as his legs could carry him. His sword was trembling in his hand.

Julia was ahead of him, Julia the Strig… no, it was his imagination. The shadow of her was gone.

He ran, and as he ran he saw more and more, as his eyes adjusted to the darkness and the dim light grew closer.

"Halt!" the shout of the soldier was dimmer now. "Halt this! More charges will be added! You will be expelled from the legions…"

But his voice was weaker, and indicated he had no intention of following Publius' filth-filled path.

And so Publius continued to run, to sprint, to splash.

The light was coming from the edges of a door.

Publius heaved himself onto a stone platform that rose above the muck. He laid his hands on the doorknob.

His body was stinking and splashed with excrement.

Yet he could see, amid the dim light that on the door a red hand was painted.

It was now or never. He could not help but feel that this was his destiny.

He twisted the doorknob and ripped it free. He plunged into the room, sword in hand.

# Chapter Thirty-Five

*Varius Tycho, Imperial Guard*

Tycho was entering Eioli again, but this time, he was doing it openly, without any deceit.

He was following the footsteps of Agatho Lornodoris, with a dozen other bodyguards. He was one among many. But among the bodyguards, only he had been chosen for his task.

He felt underneath his cloak for the knife; it was still there. He could not help himself.

His body was covered in icy sweat. His breathing had become shallow. Though what he was doing was sanctioned by the state, though what he was doing was for the Empire, he could not help but feel that killing an old man—an Imperial citizen at that— was wrong.

Yet he would honor his oath. He would honor the state that he had pledge his life to defend.

But he could not help feel nervous, and as the dark buildings—stained from below-ground with soot—emerged, and the foreign architecture became visible, the onion domes and pointed arches, he felt helpless. There was darkness in the air, a foul spirit, and fear was all about him. His fingers trembled as he felt for the knife again.

It was there, though he hadn't wanted it to be.

# Chapter Thirty-Six

*Publius Allius Corvus, Legionary*

He swept into the room, wielding his sword as if it were a flaming brand.

The room was draped with red curtains and he staggered back in horror.

On the uneven flagstone there were bodies, some gasping with life—men and women garbed in red, stabbed multiple times, with their viscera exposed.

And in front of him was Maria Domina, a face he recognized from the advertisement as Vitellia Procula.

Cold she was, and pale, and her hair was raven black. A shattered staff was lying next to her.

A man had her by the neck, a man garbed in black.

Was it a government agent? Publius could only guess.

He heard a hiss; in the corner of the room he could see Julia the Strig, hair a pallid shade of white, her black eyes filled with hate. More men were there with her, men garbed in black wielding holy symbols of silver.

"Go!" shouted the man holding Vitellia Procula's neck. "Do your duty! A Strig can only be healed by the death of the one who changed her."

Then why wasn't he killing her? Why hadn't he done it himself?

It did not make sense. Vitellia Procula looked terrified; her bony cheeks were white, her dark eyes were shallow, and she was trembling all over.

The way Publius was raised, harming a woman was the ultimate dishonor.

But then he looked once more upon Julia. He looked into

her dark eyes, black marbles. Vitellia Procula had done this to her…
Vitellia Procula, who called herself Maria Domina.

Anger rose, though he did not know where it came from;
anger rose and propelled him forward.

Publius brandished his sword, charging forward. Vitellia
screamed but it was too late; he had pierced her, and now she was
slinking to the ground, and Publius was filled with regret.

Julia had fallen to the ground; she was spasming on the
floor, shaking and screeching.

The black-garbed agents were shouting orders among
themselves.

The one holding Vitellia Procula released her body. "Well
done," he said. "Of thirteen, only you arose… of thirteen, only you
were selected."

What did he mean?

Vitellia Procula was dying on the floor. The black-garbed
agents were fleeing.

And what was going on? What was meant by this? Who
were these people?

His sword was dripping with blood.

# Chapter Thirty-Seven

*Varius Tycho, Imperial Guard*

The gate of Eioli's palace was massive, stylized with horns and faced with statues of bulls.

Fear was rising up in Tycho, terrible fear, and everywhere he looked it seemed there was a dark shadow, a menacing spirit.

The skies were bright, but there was darkness here.

Over the streets it seemed there was a fog, or perhaps smoke but he did not smell it—it did not burn his nostrils.

And out of this fog, out of the dimness of the torches, figures were beginning to take shape.

The King of Eioli was making his presence known.

He was riding on a massive cart, a cart whose every inch was covered in a bull's head. Each bull's head was layered with gold, and the cart had three levels, on top of which the king sat on his seat.

He was slight, even slender, perhaps three-fourths Tycho's height. He was not remarkable at all; plain, even, he was, dark of skin and dark of eye but looking like one of the masses of Ugars.

A crown was on his head, a crown of seven tiers, alternating gold and silver. Each tier was studded with a different gemstone— ruby and sapphire and emerald he could tell, but others had multiple colors, and one the color of a rainbow.

A trumpet blew, blasting in its intensity. Gongs were struck.

And the King of Eioli began to descend, walking down the steps from the cart.

Here he was, the man who had evaded and beguiled the Imperials for more than a year. And his plain appearance hid his cunning and devious mind.

"Bow!" His guards were approaching from the corners of

the cart—his guards were rounding the corner, and shouting. "Bow to the Great King!

"Bow to he, the Hammer of Belpheor!"

Agatho Lornodoris fell prostrate.

Tycho did not have time to feel disgust.

From the folds of his pocket he drew the knife so slender, so tiny it easily evaded detection.

"Rise!" the king shouted and Agatho Lornodoris did just that.

It was appalling to see an Imperial bow before this tyrannical potentate, but Tycho had to focus on the mission at hand, the task that had been assigned.

An attendant was coming, a woman wearing a diadem. She was bearing a tablet overlain with parchment.

"We have come to an agreement," the King said.

Another woman met her from the other side of the cart, bearing an ink-dripping quill.

"But first… you shall sing a song to Belpheor."

"That was not agreed," Agatho said. "But I shall do it."

He took the quill in his hands. He was ready to sign.

Tycho uttered a prayer under his breath.

"Ya Belpheor… Ya Belpheor…" The king began to sing. "Ya Belpheor…"

Tycho lurched forward. He hesitated.

One of Lornodoris' bodyguards looked at him incredulously.

"Ya Belpheor!" Agatho said.

And at the word Tycho leapt upon him, plunging his knife into his back. Blood began to spurt, spraying all over, but he stabbed again and Lornodoris let out the most wretched scream Tycho had ever heard.

He stabbed a third time. Now he was drenched.

Panic overtook the camp, the king, his guards, the women.

And Tycho was running, running, running down the street, as fast as he could, as fast as he could possibly go.

~

At the gate of the city he heard his fellow bodyguards shouting: "They have betrayed us! The king's men have killed our legate!"

And around Tycho's neck a garrote was pulled. Just before the city gate, he found himself unable to breathe as the garrote was pulled tighter.

"Why…" Tycho tried to say. "What…"

He did not understand what he was witnessing. He did not understand what had gone on.

The air began to leave him. He collapsed. And the last thing he saw was Sextus standing above him, Sextus, with a smile on his face.

# Chapter Thirty-Eight

*Varius Tycho, Imperial Guard*

Sextus was a killer! Sextus was a murderer.
And Tycho had been betrayed…

# Chapter Thirty-Nine

*Publius Allius Corvus, Legionary*

Publius was carrying Julia in his arms, Julia—the one the people of Imperial City had erroneously called a "princess."

He wished it were in better circumstances he were carrying her, through this tunnel dark and damp, full of stench and excrement.

But her shaking had ceased; her tremors had finally ended. Now, she was breathing lightly in his arms, between coughs and light wheezes.

Tears had formed in Publius' eyes, tears that he had done what he set out to do. He had completed his oath, the oath no less sacred than his soldier's oath. Julia was healed.

He came to the sewer main cover, where a ladder lay.

The man of the urban cohorts was gone, perhaps to get reinforcements.

Publius set Julia down on her feet. The platform beside the ladder was free of muck and excreta.

"Can you walk?" Publius said.

"I… I.." Her voice was soft and weak. "I feel… as though I've had a bad dream."

# Chapter Forty

*Vello Lychicus, Councilor*

The Council was convened and Lychicus was reading the augur's pronouncement.

"Publius Allius Corvus of Seafarers' Way," Lychicus said. "That is who shall be our emperor."

The councilors were stone-faced but the augurs' pronouncement was final.

"And yet there is something else," Lychicus said. "Something else indeed…he is not August. He does not belong to our class."

"Is he a Knight?" barked Councilor Saius.

"No," Lychicus said, "not a Knight either, but common."

The Legis was watching from the shadows. The clerk had his quill at the ready.

"A common man may not become the emperor," said Quercus, councilor from Swords Point. "It is in our laws. It is in our precedent. It has been long established that the common may not become emperor.

"Not even the augurs can change that."

"But we," said Lychicus, "may make him August. We may grant him the noble title."

"And why would we do that?" Saius said.

And like that, Lychicus knew this all would be impossible, that they would break into quarreling and argument and that there would be no end to debate, that this meeting would press on into the night without resolution.

It was what the Councilors did best… argue for the sake of arguing, debate for the sake of debate.

"And who is this Publius Allius Corvus, anyway?" Saius

said. "What makes him qualified?"

"Qualified!" Lychicus scoffed. The sun was sparkling as it shone down on the room below. "Qualified… His qualifications are irrelevant. The augur order has spoken.

"Signor Legis!" he continued. "I move to vote on a law of three parts… that we elevate the Corvus family to August status, that we nominate him, and that firstly, we find him!"

# Chapter Forty-One

*Publius Allius Corvus, Legionary*

Julia lifted the manhole cover. She managed to climb out, to take a few steps, and then she fainted.

Publius clambered out himself, into the bright sunlight. The rain had dissipated and the sun was shining through the clouds.

And people were standing about, gawking at them.

Publius scooped Julia up into his arms. It was surprisingly easy; all that legionary's training seemed to have paid off.

"Julia?" an onlooker said. "Julia? Is that Julia Seánus?"

# Interlude II

The Red Lord was enraged, standing amid the crowds of Imperial Square.

He had been right, all along.

To be turned into a Strig was torture, most certainly, but there were more important things than revenge.

"I curse you!" he said to Vitellia Procula, or Maria Domina as she liked to call herself.

"I curse you!" he said again, but he was drowned out by cheers of joy and exaltation.

The people lingering in Imperial Square were glowing; they were overwhelmed by the good news.

But bad news was coming, yes, bad news for them—the worst of all.

For the Red Dawn was now at hand.

# Chapter Forty-Two

*Julia Seánus*

What happened?

As Publius carried her through the halls of the Imperial Palace, she realized she did know, she did know what had happened and what she had done.

She knew more than she wanted to know.

There were pictures on the wall, pictures of Imperial heroes, of Anthans the Conqueror, of Valerius the Kingslayer.

Yes, she knew what she had done… and now she was weak.

She could feel her consciousness fading.

~

She came to in a room whose contours she recognized.

But her bedroom had been stripped bare.

Besides the bed, off in the corner, the silken curtains were gone, the rugs vanished, baring the hardwood floor.

She was on a divan, lying on her back. Publius was crouching beside her, sitting on a stool, touching her hair.

If he knew what she had done, he wouldn't be looking at her like that.

# Chapter Forty-Three

*Publius Allius Corvus, Legionary*

The Seánus family was synonymous with opulence; it was as ancient as it was wealthy, as ancient as it was highly revered.

And Julia, scion of its most notable branch, was looking at Publius like he was a hero, as if he were Phillipidēs or Helēmon of old.

Yes, she was looking at Publius Corvus of Seafarers' Way like that.

But there was a hidden sadness in her eyes as well. And it seemed there were unsaid words hovering on the tip of her tongue.

"Julia," Publius said. "You have been through much."

"And I have done much," Julia answered.

Publius only looked at her a while.

He knew it was true.

He knew a little of what she had done.

He wondered if there was more.

For she had joined the Red Hand cult, the cult that had assassinated her father. She had falsified her abduction.

Yes, she had done much, but that was the past. Would the Imperial Council see it differently?

# Chapter Forty-Four

*Varius Tycho, Legionary*

Tycho gasped for air.

And when he gasped, he could taste blood in his mouth, and on his tongue.

His hands and feet were bound with rope.

He was on a high platform. There were Ugars behind him and Ugars below.

He was in Eioli.

Sextus had failed to kill him.

There was a statue in front of him, a great blazen statue, a statue of Belpheor. It was so superheated the bronze had turned a radiant gold. Even at a distance, it was charring his skin.

Below them was an Ugar priest, riling up the crowds.

Tycho screamed.

"A sacrifice!" the priest shouted. "A sacrifice to Belpheor! For he loves Imperial blood best!"

He cursed them; he cursed Eioli.

"Eioli! Eioli, you will fall!" Tycho shouted, just as they tossed him from the platform, just as he plunged toward the statue's molten hands.

# Part Three

# Chapter Forty-Five

*Vello Lychicus, Councilor*

The young man was before them, standing before the council.

He was a legionary of no especial note.

Dark was his hair, and dark were his eyes. He was muscular and hale. He was young, not yet thirty. And he was strong.

But Lychicus could tell the councilors were not convinced. He could tell they would not go through with this; no, they would use his nomination as an excuse to convene the council, to circumvent the Legis' rules and carry on the affairs of the government.

"What," said Saius, "is your name?"

"Publius Allius Corvus."

"And do you know, Signor Corvus, why you are here?" Saius said.

"I do not know," Publius said. "I do not…"

"That is apparent," Saius said. "For if you knew, you would have done more to impress us."

Lychicus viewed Publius, a lone figure standing below the countless rows of councilors. The oculus was shining through.

He was common, of no special talent. But he seemed smart enough, capable enough.

And he had rescued the emperor's daughter. She had been plucked from captivity.

Publius had done this. How could the councilors not respect him?

# Chapter Forty-Six

*Julia Seánus*

Julia watched from the shadows.

When she was a little girl, she had watched the proceedings of the Imperial Council with emotions that ranged from total boredom to complete hostility.

Now she could see Publius there, Publius who had rescued her.

They were questioning him, and everything would be on record, for the public to see if they wanted to see it.

And she had seen such questionings before. She knew what this method of interrogation meant, though Publius did not.

They were trying to see if he was fit for the White Throne.

# Chapter Forty-Seven

*Publius Allius Corvus, Legionary*

Publius did not belong in these majestic halls.

Of all these councilors, it seemed the blond one was the most hostile towards him.

He could not believe the opulence, the masonry, the crenellations and abstract carvings that ran up the length of the dome. The marble floor was pristine, swept clean and layered with beeswax. He could not have imagined this moment, and he did not understand it.

"I repeat," Saius said. "Do you know why you are here?"

He supposed he had to guess.

"Because I rescued Julia Seánus?" Publius offered.

But he had not truly rescued her; he felt there were forces that had led him to her.

Did they think it was he who had kidnapped her? Did they think he had done this to her, kept her in prison in the sewers? Did they think he had been holding her for ransom?

"We thank the gods for Julia's rescue," the blond man said. "And you, no doubt, played a great part. But that is not why you are here, Publius Allius Corvus, and I fear for that very reason you are not worthy of this meeting."

It was a meeting, a convening of the council, a process he never thought he'd witness.

He was a man of Mud Bottom, the son of a tailor. All these old men, peering high above him in their finely carved seats, were Augusts. They were noblemen and he was common.

"Publius Allius Corvus," the blond man said, "tell me, if you were to sit on the White Throne, how would you govern?"

The question was outrageous. How could they ask him

that?

An old man spoke instead, the oldest and most decrepit looking among them. As he rose, he leaned on a cane. The blond man sat down.

"Publius," he said.

The informality was welcome.

"You are here because the augur order has chosen you to be our next emperor."

But why? It did not make sense.

Thoughts began to percolate in his head, a mélange of memories. Who were those black-garbed agents in the sewers? They had led him to Julia.

And why would the augurs—sorcerers of wind and speed—choose him?

"How would I govern?" Publius was speaking before he was thinking. "I would crush the Empire's enemies. I would expand the Empire to its maximal extent."

"Do not tell us what you think we want to hear," the old man said. "And when you address us, address us by our names."

"I do not know your names," Publius said.

"Then you did not come prepared," the old man answered, "and for that reason I fear Signor Saius is right. You are unready and ill equipped for the task."

Publius never claimed he wasn't. He hadn't asked for this. And he still did not understand it.

"Signor—"

"Lychicus," the old man said. "That is my name. And we know yours. We fear you are unready. But tell me, Publius, in your truest self, how would you govern? If you were to sit upon the White Throne, what would you do? Speak from your heart."

"I—I"

"Answer us," said Lychicus. "Much rests on this question."

"I would retreat to our shores," Publius said. "I would

withdraw."

"You would allow your enemies to encroach? You would abandon our allies?" Lychicus said.

"No—"

"It is a good an answer as any," Lychicus said. "But I have questioned many candidates.

"And I can tell, deep in your heart, that that is not what you would do. No, you would not call in our soldiers. You would not retreat to our shores."

There was a long pause.

"Tell me, Publius, is the emperor a king?"

"No—" he started.

"No, he is not," Lychicus said. "For his powers come from the Imperial Council, and their powers come from the people. The emperor is not a king. He is far more powerful than a king. He commands the armies and none are permitted to disobey him.

"That is why I believe you are unready. The matter is not decided. But I move that we recess. I move that this session is over."

A man in strange leather clothes—leggings and a jerkin— wearing a red-crested soldier's helm on his head—strode forward.

"The council has made a motion to adjourn. The Legis will call the roll."

The sting of humiliation hung all about Publius. And though he had never asked for this, though it hadn't been his desire, still the words hurt him, still their penetrating questions wounded his ego.

He walked away, not knowing where to go. He was soon joined in the halls by Julia.

~

Past marble corridors lined with busts and statues, beyond ivory statuettes and paintings whose color seemed to fluoresce in the candlelight, Publius walked in Julia's company.

"I feel like a fool," Publius said. "But I'm not… I'll prove it to them."

"You should have seen my father's questioning," Julia said. She stopped near an alcove where there was a statue of Amara, the mother goddess.

Her blue eyes were radiant in the light of the windows. She had recovered fully. She was who she had been when they'd first met, when she had appeared to him in visions.

And questions returned to Publius, questions that had lingered not far beneath the surface.

# Chapter Forty-Eight

*Julia Seánus*

She had not told him how she found him, how the dark temple on the lonely mountain had caused her to fear the nation she had loved.

He still did not know why he'd been taken there. He still did not know what the temple was.

He did not know that her actions—though unintentional—had led him to this place, to the very White Throne.

# Chapter Forty-Nine

*Publius Allius Corvus, Legionary*

"Where to begin?" Julia said.

She was lying on the divan in her bedroom. Outside, rain was pouring down. Winter had come like a flood; the storm had been raging for hours, and the Council had not met in days.

"Where to begin?" Julia said, and this time her voice was softer, weaker, more filled with grief. "Oh, Publius. I do not think I will be long for this world. When the Council meets, and find out what I did… well, even the August are not above the law."

"Tell me," Publius said. "You can tell me anything. You know that."

Thrice they had made love, though it was fornication, though Julia had initially been reluctant. Marriage between Augusts and the common was rare. She had asked about it already, but Publius wasn't sure.

"I know I can tell you anything," Julia said. "But I fear you will not look at me the same."

There was a pause, and Publius did not object. He only waited to hear her tell the tale.

"It may surprise you that many Augusts do not think highly of our country. But that was not at the root of my fear of the Empire, of my own nation, which soon turned to passionate loathing.

"It was those Augusts… it was the Cult of the Blighted One. It was my fear of what the Empire will one day become.

"When my friends told me about the Cult of the Red Hand, I had already begun to doubt our nation… to see its actions as motivated by self-interest and oppression.

"The Cult of the Red Hand believes that when the emperor

dies, the true emperor… the Red Lord… will appear. The Empire will fall, the skies will turn as blood. The world will be remade.

"And though I did not believe it, I sympathized with their goals, for by then my chats in Paradise Gardens, my conversations with my friends in the City, had turned my loathing for the Empire into hatred.

"I hated it so much that when the Red Hand demanded I leave, that I stage my abduction, that I went through with it… though I knew it was part of a plot to kill my father. It was part of a plot to usher in the Red Dawn. And though I told myself and tried to convince myself my motivations were innocent, deep down I knew…. Deep down I knew what I was doing would lead to my father's death."

Publius was only watching her silently. He had already suspected this. He had already surmised it from what she had told him. He had already forgiven her, though it was not his to forgive.

"And so my next task was to find the Red Lord… not to find the Red Lord, but to *make* a Red Lord. And I tried to call you."

It didn't make sense. But he was glad, all that time ago, that he refused to do what she wished.

"But I did make a Red Lord in the Marshal of the Guard… Tidus Sulpicius Varro… and he took to his new role with relish."

"You *made* him?" Publius said. He remembered the figure he had seen standing in the crowds of Imperial Square, and what the tribune Gnaius had said—that he had borne the insignia of the Imperial Guard.

"I made him," Julia said, "for that was what Maria Domina… sorry, Vitellia… wanted. She wanted to make a Red Lord, because she knew the Red Lord would not appear on his own.

"By then I was in too deep to get out. Once I failed to convince you, I remembered Tidus Varro. He had come in to a tavern in the Suburro searching for me… I had been in the shadows. And when you had said no, I thought he was a prime target, for he was devoted to me.

"Or so I thought…"

Publius looked upon her. The sunlight was lying lightly upon her hair; her lips were luscious and red. He touched her hand.

She gazed into his eyes.

"He became convinced more than I ever was. He began to hate the Empire he had served. He truly believed he was the Red Lord and not a tool in Maria Domina's hands.

"You see, Maria is not an Imperial. She had reasons to hate the Empire. Her mother was a Geat, a native of this peninsula. But Tidus… Tidus was an Imperial through and through, a servant of it. He had no reasons to be consumed with such zeal.

"And that zeal caused them both to turn on me… because my name is Seánus. Because I was the emperor's daughter. Because my family and my name has been a part of the Empire since its founding.

"I believe they always planned to turn on me. They would use my gift to their advantage and then destroy me.

"And so Maria Domina, a necromancer, cast a spell on me. And that is the last I remember before I saw you."

"You were… changed," Publius said. "You were not yourself. But you still seemed to have memories. You were pursuing me."

"Perhaps, I knew you were my hope," Julia said, "even in that state. Even in that state, I desired you."

# Chapter Fifty

*Publius Allius Corvus, Legionary*

The days droned on, and they turned into weeks.

Harsh and violent were the storms. The city seemed haunted, visited by lightning, rain and wind.

And unbeknownst to Julia, Publius had purchased a wedding ring.

Rain was pouring down, and the winds were gusting, when there was a knock on Publius' chamber door.

He walked up to it, opened it just a crack. Lychicus was standing there, Vello Lychicus, the councilor who seemed the foremost among them.

"Publius," he said, "come with me."

~

He was leaning on a cane, slightly stooped over. They were headed in the direction of the Council House.

"I have bad news," he said once they had reached the Sky Bridge. "The council is deadlocked. Paralyzed, as always. I fear your nomination will not even see a vote.

"That is the Council for you."

They stopped at the Sky Bridge.

The city below was vast. The violent rain had slowed to a trickle.

"Will you go back to the legion? We can appoint you a tribune for your troubles," Lychicus said.

"No," Publius said. "I will not go back. I will be emperor."

Lychicus smiled faintly.

The lights of the city below warmed Publius' heart. One

false step and he could go plunging all those fathoms to his death.
When he was emperor, he would build a railing.

# Chapter Fifty-One

*Vello Lychicus, Councilor*

It was a cold, dark day when the letter arrived.

It was sealed in an official seal, a slip of parchment rolled up, delivered from the Grand Legate at Eioli.

The Council was meeting today.

But it had been addressed to Lychicus, delivered to his private office. He wondered why.

He broke the seal and allowed the parchment to unravel.

# Chapter Fifty-Two

*Publius Allius Corvus, Legionary*

News arrived like a deluge; the Imperial Council was a hive of gossip and now of anger.

Angry councilors walked the halls, angry councilors filled with rage: The King of Eioli had accepted the Council's offer of peace, then murdered Agatho Lornodoris in cold blood when he had come to sign the agreement.

They had driven back the armies of the Empire; panic had once again devastated the ranks.

And one dark winter morning, Publius was summoned to the meeting of the Council.


"Tell me," Speaker Lychicus said with fury in his voice. "Tell me what you will do as emperor, if you are so named."

"Signor Speaker," said Publius, "they have driven us back again. Once more they have driven us away.

"But I tell you, distinguished Councilors, Augusts all… if I were to sit upon the White Throne, Eioli would be in my sights. She would be my chief goal.

"And if the Empire were to fall and crack and crumble, and the City to slide into the sea, we would fall and crack and crumble, and we would slide into the sea fighting Eioli. I would not rest until we are avenged."


The vote was unanimous; the Corvus name was made August. The vote was unanimous; Publius was made emperor.

# Chapter Fifty-Three

*Julia Seánus*

Julia wept at the sight of Publius.

The Silver Circlet was on his head.

He was seated where the emperor was, on the White Seat, observing the Council.

She wept at the sight of him, for she knew now he'd be in the Red Hand's sights.

And still she feared for her safety.

Still she feared Varro's men were in the palace.

Still she was afraid.

Would the Red Dawn come? Would the skies be set alight, and a new world remade, a world where there was no place for Seáni or Lornodorises?

She wept at the sight of him… Publius Allius Corvus, emperor, the leader of the Empire.

# Chapter Fifty-Four

*Emperor Publius Corvus*

The armies were being marshaled.

In the Council House, Publius sat in his place, in the White Seat, observing its proceedings.

"Two legions recalled from Kheroe…" Speaker Lychicus was saying. "One legion from the border… armaments being made…"

He was listing the preparations for the greatest and final siege of Eioli.

The doors to the Council House burst open. A herald was bringing in a letter bearing the Imperial seal.

Lychicus took the letter in his hands. He broke the seal and let it unravel.

"A report from one Varius Tycho," Lychicus said. "Let it be read into the record."

~

Gold was in Eioli, in excess of two thousand talents or more. Gold was in Eioli, and if any councilors were unconvinced of the war effort, they would be convinced now.

# Chapter Fifty-Five

*Vello Lychicus, Speaker of the Council*

Julia was missing again…. She was missing again! She had disappeared.

Would he tell Publius Corvus? Would he tell him outright?

Baleful signs there were in the heavens… the moon was ochre. The sign of the Bull was in aspect and the Eagle was in retrograde.

Where was Julia? She had to be found… She had to be found!

# Epilude

In his secret chamber, the Red Lord paced angrily.

The plot by his servant Gray Hood had failed. Julia had escaped his clutches.

But the Red Dawn was coming. The Red Dawn was coming; he knew it in his heart.

The door to the chamber burst open. Soldiers came pouring in. They tackled him. They shackled him and slammed him to the ground.

"Where is Julia?" they were shouting. "Where is Julia, Varro?"

Varro… had that been his name?

"Where is Julia?" they said again.

If only he knew…

# Glossary

**Aediles:** In Imperial City, city regulators that are charged with investigating market illegalities and public corruption.

**Anthania:** A large peninsula, with the Middle Sea on its eastern edge and the ocean on its west. It is named after Anthans the Conqueror.

**Anthans:** A famed Imperial legate who conquered much of what is now called the Anthanian Peninsula.

**Augusts:** The higher of the two tiers of Imperial nobility, with those under them being called knights. They are the descendants of the original founders of the Empire.

**Barbarian:** A derogative term for a person who is neither Imperial nor from the Eastern Kingdoms.

**Century:** The smallest division of the Imperial army, composed of about one-hundred to two-hundred men, under the command of an official called a centurion.

**Council House, the:** A tower-like structure that dominates the Imperial City skyline, its construction was begun not long after the initial conquest of the Anthanian peninsula.

**Draco:** A miniature dragon-like creature, the size of a human fist, generally red or yellow in color. They are beloved as pets, especially among the southrons.

**Eastern Kingdoms, the:** A term for the rich, ancient lands of Eloesus on the opposite shore, far east across the Middle Sea.

**Eioli:** Considered the queen city of Ugarit, it is the region's richest and most storied city. It has dominated Ugarit for centuries.

**Emperor:** The leader of the empire, taking on some of the roles of a king, but heavily checked by the power of the Imperial Council.

**Flamens:** A secretive group of sorcerers believed to have powers of invisibility and far-sight.

**Grand Legate:** The commander appointed to control several legions.

**Ghuls:** In southron legend, monstrous creatures that feast on rotten flesh. They haunt ruins in the desert and are said to sometimes venture into human villages and pluck men from the gallows.

**Imperial City:** The largest city of the Empire, considered its heart. Its legal name is Anthans, named after the conqueror of the peninsula.

**Imperial Council:** A semi-democratic branch of the Imperial government, formed by thirty men voted for by the free citizens of Imperial City's thirty wards.

**Imperial Guard:** A group of about a hundred veterans of the legions, considered an elite fighting force. They are tasked with guarding the emperor.

**Kerius:** An August family, noted for their ancient history. The forefather of the Kerius family, Fido Kerius, was a war hero in the time before the Unification.

**Kheroe:** A city-state directly south of the Anthanian peninsula, across the sea. It is known for its strange customs and its ancient wealth. They are one of the oldest of the Empire's allies.

**Knight:** The lower of two tiers of the Imperial nobility. Traditionally they were seen as the Empire's soldiers, but that distinction has faded. Now, many of the Knightly class have no connections to the military.

**Lateran War:** A minor war in the northeastern region of Anthania, Latera, that began with barbarian raids and led to Latera's unsuccessful secession from the Empire.

**Legate:** The commander of a legion.

**Legion:** The largest division of the Imperial armies, composed of around five thousand men.

**Middle Sea, the:** An immense sea in the center of the world. The Empire lies on its westernmost edge.

**Paradise Gardens:** A resort town for the rich in the foothills of the Goldenhorn Mountains. Members of the Imperial Council often retreat there at the height of summer.

**Ratlings:** Furry humanoids that superficially resemble rats. They are rumored to spread disease, but this rumor has never been substantiated.

**Seladora:** The goddess of woodlands, the gentle side of nature, and nymphs.

**Suburro:** A poor ward of Imperial City, located just outside Imperial Square.

**Ugar:** A native of the land of Ugarit.

**Ugarit:** A land on the Anthanian peninsula's west-central coast, dominated by the three cities of Eioli, Tikal and Hoda. They are noted for their customs that are very different from the other people groups of the peninsula.

**Unification. the:** Considered one of the founding events of the Empire, the Unification occurred when the Formusus and Tenebarius tribes united under one king, establishing a kingdom on the island of Peregoth. A series of seven kings, called by some the Sea Kings, ruled until they were overthrown and a semi-democratic system was formed.

# About the Author

Cursed at birth with a wild imagination, Andrew Cooper spent his youth dreaming of worlds more exciting than Earth.

He is a graduate of the Odyssey Writing Workshop. His stories have appeared in Morpheus Tales, Fear and Trembling, Residential Aliens and Mindflights, among others.

# Contact the Author

Visit **www.aj-cooper.com** to sign up for the newsletter and stay up-to-date on new releases.

Find him on Facebook at:

**www.facebook.com/AJCooperauthor**

www.ingramcontent.com/pod-product-compliance
Lightning Source LLC
Chambersburg PA
CBHW031237210726
48287CB00003B/807